Darpan

Stories of Indian Women in Transition

The Indian woman in a myriad roles and situations is reflected in this collection of stories. Marriage and companionship, rebellion and conformity, unconditional love and acceptance and the changes wrought by time are all brought alive with fine brush strokes to present a complex picture of womanhood.

Sesh Rao Damerla has worked for many years as a teacher and trainer to upgrade the language and soft skills of students and managers in order to move from efficiency to effectiveness. She has been associated with NGOs that work for the upliftment of women, such as SPECTRUM, a ladies study group, Ashraya, Friends of Children and Akanksha. Her experiences provided the ideal ingredients for her development as a writer, as she learnt to observe, analyse and understand human behaviour and psychology. The present collection of stories brings out her ability to depict themes and situations that readers will be able to identify with, with the sensitivity and imagination they deserve.

Darpan

Stories of Indian Women in Transition

Sesh Damerla

VISHWAKARMA
PUBLICATIONS VP

Darpan
Stories of Indian Women in Transition

Edition - October 2015
© Sesh Damerla

ISBN 978-93-83572-63-2

Published by:
Vishwakarma Publications
283, Budhwar Peth, Near City Post,
Pune- 411 002.
Phone No: (020) 20261157 / 24448989
Email: info@vpindia.co.in
Website: www.vpindia.co.in

Cover Design
Meghnad Deodhar

Typeset and Layout
Gold Fish Graphics, Pune.

Printed at
Repro India Limited,
Mumbai

Dedication

To my dear mother who is my inspiration

Smt. Rajyalakshmi Kanakraj

Readers' Voices...

'Darpan: Stories of Indian Women in Transition' is truly absorbing. Indeed, I found this book eminently readable and insightful.

In the book, there is a wide diversity of characters of Indian Women, that are portrayed by the author Sesh Damerla. They range from poor to the neo-rich, from those that are suppressed and victimised to those that triumph over adversity showing exceptional courage and character, and also from those that merely survive to those that have the urge to succeed, and who do succeed. These characters, be it Amita, Milli, Chandra, Meena, Kusum... all of them come alive because of the interesting "story telling" style of Sesh Demerla.

Bharat Ratna Maharshi Dhondo Keshav Karve had made a profound statement 'Sanskrita Stree Parashakti', meaning that an enlightened woman is a source of infinite strength. An enlightened and educated woman can achieve ultimate empowerment.

I was the President of Indian Science Congress in the year 2000. In my Presidential speech in Pune I had proposed a 'New Panchsheel for New Millennium'. It was all about just five points; Child Centered Education, Woman Centered Society, Human Centered Development, Knowledge Centered Society and Innovation Centered India.

I quote from the points that I had made about creating a woman centered Indian society. 'Human Development Report 1992 had said' 'No country treats its women as well as its men' Can the India of the next millennium afford to stand on only one of its legs? A woman has to be allowed the full expression of her potential and she has to be empowered to become a dynamic partner in the building of the new India of our dreams.

As Nobel Laureate Aung San Sun Kyi had said 'In societies, where men are truly confident of their own worth, women are not nearly tolerated, but valued'. It is this change of value system, that will lead to the eventual empowerment of woman. In this context, the book beautifully brings out the challenge of empowerment of an India woman, and what it could mean for our society, and indeed for our nation.

Anais Nin had said 'How wrong is it for a woman to expect the man to build the world she wants, rather than to create it herself?' As Sesh Damerla points out 'my stories attempt to reflect a majority of women for whom transition has been an upward movement from total dependence on a man to survival, and further on to empowerment, be it total or partial'. And she is absolutely right here.

I am sure the readers will find this collection of stories of an 'Indian woman in transition' both informative and inspirational.

Dr. R. A. Mashelkar
National Research Professor

"Story telling has always proved to be the finest way of messaging subtly. These stories make the reader aware of how influenced in our attitudes we are by the lenses we have on our eyes. The other half of humanity is about to be released from its traditional status. A subtle change is going on. Bravo to Sesh Damerla"

R. Gopalakrishnan,
Director, Tata Sons Ltd.

"It is often said, that men cannot understand women. It is true to some extent, but if women can write so beautifully and express the women in her, men can at least come close to a woman's thinking.... Sesh has done that with her wonderful work – Darpan (yes, a mirror to oneself)

I was born in a Nair family, where a woman is head of the family and more empowered than in most Indian communities. But understanding women from different perspectives was also important to me.

Sesh has done a wonderful job by bringing in many aspects of a woman in such a simple and profound manner. These stories are not just short and easy to read, but also profound in nature.

One cannot but associate with each of the characters as if it was one's own mother, sister, wife or daughter. I felt like a woman, as I was reading through these stories. Maybe, making me a better man.

I suggest that let this book be called a family book rather than a women's book. Let each family read a story and discuss and share those emotions, feelings and learnings. Thus making each other respect and appreciate each other.

Sesh has an amazing way of storytelling, the way it is told in our Indian tradition. Stories are a way to a person's heart and feelings. But each story has a different moral for every person.

Radhakrishnan Pillai
Director,
Chanakya Institute of Public leadership (CIPL),
Department of Philosophy, University of Mumbai.

"A book that talks about life as it is for every woman in this country."

Sudha Menon
Author of *Legacy* and *Gifted*.

This is a collection of captivating stories in contemporary Indian setting, narrated in an easy, flowing and charming style of storytelling. Covering a wide array of what seems like real life situations, every reader – of any gender or age – can relate instantly with the characters in the tales. For me, this induced a sense of participation in the events unfolding in the stories; and made it great fun to read them!

Ms Sesh Damerla truly has wonderful expression and an ability to connect with readers through her characters. Her stories reveal that she has an insightful understanding of the transition that is taking place in our societies today; and of the attitudinal ambiguities such changes inevitably bring with them. Are we responding of our free will to such changes? Or are we responding through our traditional conditioning and societal pressures? Her stories hold up an excellent mirror.

R V Krishnan
Founder
BDB India Private Limited

"At last, we have a vibrant new author on the Indian scene! Sesh Rao Damerla eloquently weaves tales around the various vicissitudes faced by an Indian woman and how she rises to the occasion, undaunted by her circumstances. Be it a Chandra who literally faces a 'life and death situation' or Paranjala the canny but sensitive politician or the courageous Sabina or even Mani who grabs life with both hands! The ethos that echoes in each and every story is heartfelt and will surely convince the reader that there is more to her than meets the eye! 'Darpan-Indian Women in Transition' is an absolute must read and is probably something that everyone could relate to, in their own way.

What a wonderful read! Sesh Rao Damerla's "heroines" absolutely fascinated me. They are real, they are strong and any woman, of any age or strata, can easily relate to them.

Geeta Monga
Engineer and home maker.

Going through Darpan one tends to connect with it instantly. The stories are so well written that they touch a chord in your heart somewhere, making you relive the moments and a realization sets in. Sesh has well brought out the changing patterns of one's behavior and attitude as one grows in life. The stories are not elitist but in fact speak of women from all walks of life right from the rural to the urban. The simplicity of the language and free flowing words bring a realization of the harsh truth faced by women from all walks of life. With her stories Sesh has conveyed a true understanding of the personal and intimate problems that women from different strata of our multifarious society face and how they overcome them. This book can inspire many of us and make us realize the strength we all possess within.

Dolly Manghat
Astrologer and international motivational speaker

Acknowledgements

A Big Thank You

From the minute one starts penning one's thoughts to seeing the book on the stands it is unquestionably a very highly exciting and compelling process. This process is never complete without the support of many people at different stages. Here, I would like to say a big thank you to each one of them. But for them Darpan would not have been launched.

At the outset I would like to salute all those people, men and women whose lives inspired me to create my characters in the collection of short stories titled, Darpan. I found many of them in my family fold and others were those whom I met in college, in the army circles and while working as a consultant and visiting faculty. They could never have dreamt they would be a part of my book and will become known to my readers. Fiction is based on a fair amount of reality.

To start with I would like to say a Big Thank You to the editorial team at Vishwakarma Publications. Thank you Scharada, Vishal and Shraddha.

I am extremely thankful to the ladies and gentlemen who gave their precious time to read Darpan and give their invaluable and highly encouraging comments. Thank you Ms Dolly Manghat, Ms Geeta Monga, Mr Gopalakrishnan, Dr Radhakrishnan Pillai, Dr Raghunath Mashelkar, Mr RV Krishnan and Ms Sudha Menon.

Thank you Sunanda Mehta for writing the Foreword.

I appreciate the efforts of Amod Inamdar and Sandhya Mandore in enhancing the quality of my social media inputs.

Finally no venture is possible without the support of one's family. Thank you Nani, my husband, my daughters Deepika and Swapna, my son-in-law Rajesh and my grandchildren Sharmeila and Rahil.

Sesh Damerla

Foreword

Do you know the 20 things a woman should stop wearing after 30? The answer: 1-20 the weight of other people's expectations and judgments.

This was a text I received just the other day.

These were also the words that ran through my mind as I turned the pages of this book- reading, mulling over and absorbing each of the 14 stories that, so true to the book's title, mirror the changing image of the Indian woman- right from her roles and responsibilities as a woman to the rediscovery and redefining of her own identity.

The world around us has changed dramatically over the past two decades- thanks to the advent of information technology that has broken down global walls and encompassed the entire human race into one virtual world. While the ramifications of this new age advancement are manifold, nowhere perhaps has this been a bigger catalyst for change than in the sphere of feminism. The entry of the world into our personal spaces has affected fairly rapid and successful unshackling of the fetters that had suffocated womanhood for far too long and opened up newer horizons- both in terms of opportunities and attitudes, in the physical and mental spheres.

This is especially true perhaps of my generation of women who grew up in a fairly conservative environment and found their true liberation in a world they only stepped into years later – and in many cases in step with their children. For the new world today is one that has largely freed the woman from the heaviest burden she had to carry on her shoulders- that of expectations and judgments. The world conspired to put her on a pedestal only to in turn demand of her an unending line of sacrifices and compromises. A pedestal that she reluctantly ascended, for she knew that once on it she dare not rock the balance with the added weight of her own ambitions and aspirations in life.

It is this burden which has now shifted with the times, allowing the women in India to breathe of the freedom they hitherto only learnt of during their childhood through books and stories, but which they saw becoming increasingly elusive as they stepped into adulthood and into the traditional roles laid down by society's diktats.

Darpan reflects that change in the air. Be it the contrast between the obedient Anju and the rebel Milli and how life evens out the difference in Prateeksha, the miscalculations of Ameeta in How Was She To Know or the hidden strength of Chandra in The Dilemma. The stories talk of how a woman can handle loss (Neela in Merry Wives at a party and Moni in The Baby's First Step), parental responsibilities (Munni in Rakhee) and a redefined sense of life's surprises (Kusum in Feelings). Most significantly what leaves a lasting impression on you are that the stories are told at a leisurely pace, devoid of melodrama and are more of narratives from the book called Life rather than stereotyped stories that need to have a structured format and an ending where all the loose ends tie up. In many of the stories in fact, the end is left open to interpretation, making this both a compelling read and a thought provoking experience. And if there is anything that does tie it all together it's the sublime message that the only thing that works as far as liberation of the women is concerned is the right to take their own decisions in life and thus control their destinies. Some may be right, some may be wrong but the power to steer your life in a certain way, sans guilt, is what real freedom is all about. It's the true Darpan of our ultimate evolution as a species.

Sunanda Mehta
Resident Editor, The Indian Express

Introduction

The theme of my collection of fourteen stories is the Indian Woman in Transition.

Each of the three words has a strong connection with the topics I have chosen. They say it all. Indian women, like all others the world over, are being intensely impacted in more ways than one as they traverse their journey in the business of living.

The word woman is common to all members of the female species and she is endowed with similar or common traits, strengths, opportunities and weaknesses. The difference lies in the manner in which she perceives and handles the situations she has been compelled to face from time to time through the decades. This is only to be expected as one's conditioning is related to the prevailing historical, religious, social and economic factors in the country one lives in.

The word Indian limits the location of the stories to India. I have tried to bring out the many fascinating facets of women while handling the problems and solutions in democratic India and a few are set in the times the British ruled India. Yet, a reader from any country or background can easily identify and sympathise with my characters, as they have a universal appeal. That is because the problems associated with divorce, widowhood, gender inequality and many more can be seen internationally but the reactions and the steps taken to overcome the problems could be diverse and society specific.

The third word, Transition needs no explanation as it has been constantly taking place universally like the seasons follow one after the other...

The stories are not limited in any way to any one specific strata of society or any specific group. They include the nouveau riche and the baggage and complexes they carry and which reflect in their lives; the poor and the challenges of their poverty; and those who pay the price of being rational thinkers and who are not carried away by blind beliefs. A reader gets a taste of all these and much more when he or she meets the families of Amita, Milli and Chandra in the respective stories where they are the heroines.

The style of present day parenting and the approach adopted has undergone a sea change. Gone are the days when children were ostracised for taking decisions. They express their views freely and advise unhesitatingly too. But parents do not punish the children indiscriminately or take autocratic decisions... There are fireworks when discussions take place but there is almost never an attitude of 'my way or the highway'. Family life is more democratic today as compared to the era gone by. We can identify with all the people we meet in the stories, as each one faces similar situations in today's day and age in every home in different ways. Meena, while reliving her and her daughter's marriages brings out the changes in parenting and the way their life partners were chosen. The joys and heart breaks make for very interesting reading in Meena's Home. We realise in these stories, the persisting gender bias where the woman is suppressed and victimised. The sad thing is, very often a woman is a woman's enemy for multiple reasons. But there is a movement, however slow, towards making the woman a decision maker too. She takes small and big important decisions in the interest of herself and her family. She rises to the occasion whether it is mercy killing of kith and kin or inter-community or inter-religious marriages. In all the stories we see this but we see it in a more defined way in 'Feelings' where Kusum is victimised on a daily basis from birth. We admire Chandra in 'Dilemma', a remarkable wife and mother. Women have come out of their shells in all spheres of life and have perfected the art of being superwomen at all levels, intellectual, educational and domestic, without neglecting their traditional roles. 'The Mango Orchard' has been included though it is a little different to the main thread that runs through the other stories. It is a reminder to us that man and woman have both evolved, though at a different pace. Their very natures are different and their reactions too. Here, in Mango Orchard, we don't see the man as a dictator and suppressor but one who is human and loving as a brother, son and husband. Birju is extremely caring and sensitive and becomes emotional when he learns of the gory crime where his wife is the innocent victim. It shows how he comes out of his trauma thanks to his friend Mandir Lal and the employer Sethji.

Man has a long way to go in his journey of life and he has taken some steps forward. He does not live in a joint family in the shadow of his elders but asserts his choice over his field of education, the girl he marries and financial decisions. His journey is far from over before he attempts to climb the Mt. Everest of treating the woman as an equal in thought word and deed. He is changing but not as fast as we would like to see it. Gender bias is a malady that needs more drastic remedies that will see women coming of age much faster with the proactive support of men at home and in the workplace.

To conclude, my stories attempt to reflect a majority of women for whom transition has been an upward movement from total dependence on a man, to survival, and further on to empowerment, be it total or partial.

"*To call woman the weaker sex is a libel; it is man's injustice to woman. If by strength is meant brute strength, then, indeed, is woman less brute than man. If by strength is meant moral power, then woman is immeasurably man's superior. Has she not greater intuition, is she not more self-sacrificing, has she not greater powers of endurance, has she not greater courage? Without her, man could not be. If nonviolence is the law of our being, the future is with woman. Who can make a more effective appeal to the heart than woman?*"

[To the Women of India (Young India, Oct. 4, 1930)]"

— **Mahatma Gandhi**

Contents

THE DILEMMA

The sun, an orange ball of fire, appeared to be sinking into the Arabian Sea. Unlike human beings, the sun never rests. It moves on to the other side of the globe, bringing cheer and warmth to the people living there. According to ancient Hindu philosophers, the sun heralds hope, despair, success, failure, joy and sorrow, according to an individual's past karma.

Chandra, wearing an elegant wine red silk sari with an off-white gold border, came out of the Shiv-Parvati temple feeling totally at peace. The setting sun brought a strange peace. She was seventy four, and Ramu, her husband, close to eighty. She slipped her frail hand into her husband's firm one and walked towards the garden seat inside the temple courtyard. The garden had huge shade giving trees and seasonal summer flowers laid out around a big hut that gave it the look of a hermitage.

The couple wanted to rest after all the offerings and prayers to the Almighty. Chandra walked very slowly because of the bypass surgery she had undergone a month back. She was not in too great a shape. Her smiling face and chirpy voice camouflaged the weakness, aches and pains she felt. She loved life passionately and believed in living it up to the last dreg. She had no quarrels with life on any score. Instead, she counted her blessings. This was unlike many of her friends, half her age, who perpetually grumbled. Some said, "Chandra, you are so lucky. You have it all. No wonder you smile all the time!"

Dr. Ramu was still working in hospitals and teaching in two medical colleges. He, a gynaecologist, often delivered the third generation of kids in many families. He enjoyed the respect and trust of these families and was a friend, philosopher and mentor to them.

Today, the couple were seeking the blessings of the Almighty on their 60th wedding anniversary. They would have a big celebration when the children and their families came from the US the following month. Today was all theirs, to relive life and enjoy it. They held hands and Ramu said, "Chandra, you have been a marvellous wife. But for you, my life would be meaningless." Having said this, he was silent.

She replied, "Yes Ramu, sixty years is a long time, though it seems only yesterday that we were newlyweds starting our journey of bonding and togetherness. We deserve all the praise, considering today's generation thinks of separation and divorce as an option before the journey has barely begun. No patience or spirit of compromise!" She went on to opine that the institution of marriage would soon fly out of the window. He nodded and said, "Chandra, I am feeling very uneasy. Let's go home." She paled visibly and fear gripped her. She asked the guard on duty to ask their driver to get the car quickly. In minutes, the car was there. With the help of the temple staff, she got Ramu into the car.

He was gasping as he said, "Call the hospital on the mobile. Take me there." She now realised the wisdom of the children presenting her with a mobile phone on her last birthday. At that time, she had thought it was a total waste of money on her. The next thing, Ramu had become unconscious. Chandra held Ramu's hand all the way to Guppy's Hospital, which was set up by one of his students. She rubbed his chest. It was about 7:30 pm when they got there.

The minute they reached the hospital, the staff swung into action and put Ramu in the Intensive Care Unit. After an hour or so, the team of doctors told Chandra that he was in a very critical condition. The brain, in all probability, was dead. He was being kept alive on the life-support system. The doctors were all well-known to Ramu and Chandra. One of Ramu's students, Mohan, held Chandra's hand and said she should inform their kids. He offered to do it for her, and she nodded and handed the mobile to him.

Within a few minutes of hospitalisation, friends came in and helped her throughout the night. Their daughter Pushpa and her family came within three hours. Their son Pavan, who was in India, flew down and reached them by morning and Puneet, who lived abroad, arrived twenty-two hours later. They held their mother's hand as she gave them a run down on all that had happened.

The children admired their mother for the way she had handled the crisis with no outward show of devastation. The matter of fact way in which she recounted the unpalatable tidings of Ramu's situation made her go up several notches in the children's eyes. After all, it was not easy for anyone to accept that their life partner was unlikely to ever recover from their coma.

Each of the children consulted the doctors attending their father independently. They were told there was no hope and it was for the family to decide if they wanted to continue with the support system or not, and how long they wanted to wait. Even in their wildest dreams, the children had not bargained for this situation where they had to take a strange but crucial decision. It was not easy to say, "Okay, my father should be allowed to leave this world in peace."

Sometimes, the thought of their parents dying in the distant future did cross the children's minds when they attended the last rites of their friends' family members or their elderly relatives. They sat in pin drop silence now, totally immersed in their thoughts as Ramu lay breathing heavily with the help of the ventilator. His left hand had the intravenous drip through which he was being fed and given medicines. His eyes were shut. He looked so small in that large bed. The man who had brought cheer to so many families as a doctor, lay today, helpless in the hands of those whom he had taught to handle life, sickness and how to convey the sad news of a patient's death to the bereaved family in the hospital.

Pushpa looked at her father, lying terribly helpless in the jaws of death, and tears rolled down her face. She was the youngest in the family and the most doted on, too. Her mind went back to her babyhood and the photograph of her father lifting her up really high in the air while playing with her. She remembered her teens when often, he had supported her against her brothers. Unfairly at times! As memories flooded through her mind, she smiled. She recollected her father's tear-filled eyes as he did the kanyadan (giving away of the bride). Misery was written all over his face then.

Her mind flashed back to the night when Adi was to be born. The doctors had told Ramu not to risk delivering his grandchild. He had said, "No one dare stop me. I will make sure my grandchild says,'My doctor grandfather brought me into this world.'" She had tried to coax him during labour,to not take chances. But he hadn't heeded anyone and had brought Adi to her and said, "Little one, my grandson will be proud of me!"

She suddenly came out of her dream world to address the present crisis. "What do we do? How long do we wait? Till the body gives up and rejects the support system and he quietly leaves us for a world unknown? Or do we let go now and allow him to go with dignity? If we opt for the second alternative," she argued with herself, "then the niggling thought that 'he might have come out of it and we did not give him the chance', will be with us forever.

"What will Mom think of us?" "My children are inhuman and selfish!"

"She may go with our decision," Pushpa debated further, "but may never really forgive us. Father had always worked to save life. So, do we have the right to remove the support system? It may amount to killing him.

No, that was not true. Letting a life linger on like this when he had no chance of being his old self was brutal and criminal. But would Mom view it that way?"

Puneet and Pavan looked at their darling sister and read her thoughts. Then they looked at their beloved mother who looked so helpless and tired now. But the smile that had brought comfort to each of them, almost always, was there even now when she looked at them.

Dad had always said, "Never let problems control you;let it be the other way round." The red circular mark on their mother's forehead called sindoor, the sign of all Hindu married women, seemed to glow even brighter now.

All three of them closed their eyes and saw their mother without that red mark and shuddered. Could they take it away in one second by telling the doctors in one sentence: "Doctor, let him go."

"Is that being selfish? Should we leave it to nature? Who are we to mess with life and death?" contemplated Puneet, the sentimental one.

"The doctors are doing their best. They are only human beings and have their shortcomings and limitations. They may be wrong and there is still hope for our Dad. They are waiting for our decision! With other patients I wonder if doctors are as patient. In a general hospital I am sure, in an identical situation, a choice is not given to the immediate family at all, because there is a long waiting list of sick patients who need to be admitted."

Pavan thought logically, "What would Dad have done if Mom had been in such a situation? Difficult to tell," but he thought, "Dad would have let her go at the earliest, as, what is a body without the intelligence on its face that comes from a functioning mind?"

Pushpa thought, "Should we ask Mom? No, no! How can we ask her such a question?"

But she is the most appropriate person to take this decision as children come after the life partner! She stands to lose the most. Don't we owe her at least that much - the right to decide? As if Pavan had read her thoughts, he said, "Pushpa, what do we do now?" The answer was silence. Each of them kept brooding on the problem and the vital decision. All three looked from their father to their mother, whose future would change the most. But it was a question of time.

Chandra was looking at the three agonised faces and her heart went out to them. They must be worrying about Ramu and his future.

She thought, "Who is to decide - the children, me alone or all of us? I think, as a mother I have always tried to keep them away from misery and pain, and now I can do nothing, as they are lost and helpless. Am I the reason for their misery or losing their beloved father? I guess it is a bit of both."

"I guess my life will be different from now on, as there is no hope for Ramu." She looked at the man who lay still but for the heavy breathing. Was that enough? Did she hope to see Ramu smiling and sitting on the temple seat again and saying all that was unsaid...Was it that, that was making her not take any decision? "Am I crazy to wish all this when coma means almost death? Not really, as miracles do happen. Or do they? I am a doctor's wife and I am thinking like an emotional, illiterate woman. God does not view it that way. He is testing me and He can bring him back to me. Did He not give the mythological character Savitri her husband Satyavan back, after he was dead?"

"That was only a story, Chandu," said a voice from within. She remembered the play she had seen years back,'Whose Life is it Anyway?'"Who is to take the decision? Poor Ramu can't and the children may not want to! They are our children and are not equipped to face such situations. It is Ramu's life, but may be; only I should have the right to make the decision. Living or dead, we are one, so I have to think now and no one else."

She looked at Ramu and began to laugh. Pushpa, Pavan and Puneet turned their heads and wondered if their mother had lost her mind? Pushpa put her hand on her mother's lap. Chandra said, "Push I am alright. I laughed because I imagined what your Dad is thinking now, as we sit totally in the dumps. I am sorry he can't think. Poor thing!" Her throat went dry.

Pavan admired their amazing mother and went and hugged her. Chandra thought that she couldn't make her children go through this trauma. So she got up and slowly walked to Ramu and with trembling hands touched his face and talked as if he were listening to her. "Ramu, you have always guided me and now are you testing me? That is not funny. What am I to do?" Ramu, you would have let me go in peace and dignity. I would have liked it that way. And you, Ramu?"

She wiped a tear with the back of her hand and continued to talk. "Am I being selfish by holding on to you or should I allow time to decide? Ramu, you are there now in the room at least physically. Is it enough? Yes, I can see you and touch you."

"What is the use?" said a voice from within. "His sharp and witty brain is what you admired the most."

"Even if you go physically, you will be with me mentally and guide me always. Our marriage goes far beyond the physical. Our hearts, minds and soul are linked to each other, so I should let the body go. That is the right thing." She felt then that Ramu was saying that she was his Chandu. She thought all the signs of marriage had a social significance only. They were purely man-made, for social reasons. She kissed his cheek.

Then she walked steadily to her children with courage written all over her face and said, "Children, I am alright. I give my consent to the removal of the support system. I am there always for you. Go and say your goodbyes to your Dad."

The three siblings gave their assent with their silence. They thought that their Dad had saved so many lives and here they could not save his. Puneet said aloud, "Dad, we are sorry but we know you are proud of us."

"I will inform Dr. Kumar of our decision," said Chandra to her children. "He can't live like a vegetable. I must free him from this life." She picked up her cell phone before she changed her mind and called the doctor.

"Good bye, till we meet again, Ramu, my darling," Chandra said, as the children led her to the car.

HOW WAS SHE TO KNOW?

Ameeta opened the large office window that overlooked the Arabian Sea. The light blue lace curtains flapped gently to the soft sea breeze like a dancer synchronizing his steps to the music. The sea breeze is like a music conductor. In the distance, the sea looked pretty still, and Ameeta recalled the age-old proverb, 'Still waters run deep.' How deep, she wondered, and thought - could the ocean be compared to human relationships? However long a courtship was, one could never know the true nature of one's fiancée or spouse. From her personal experience, her fiancée was willing to bring the moon to her feet but it was a different story once the sindoor (applied in the parting of a woman's hair to signify marriage during the wedding) was put in place, and the mangalsutra tied. It had been hypocrisy and nothing else!

She pondered, "Anyway, today I am at the crossroads. The quandary is, once divorced, do I have the right to seek my happiness once again? Are all men really wolves and cads? Is Sati, my admirer, deceptive, slimy and creepy like Gautam, my husband? O God! Am I losing my mind? Can't I decide for myself? Don't tell me I am a coward or worse still, a nervous wreck!"

As these thoughts buzzed in her mind, she moved away from the window to run away from this mental torture and enigma. She wanted to go to her favourite haunt where she could meditate and think straight. It was a ten-minute walk to the lonely secluded spot on the beach behind a rock. As the waves washed over her delicate feet she began to relive her life till now, to find the right solution to her life which seemed to be one big mess of confusion... Nature seemed to be her doctor, silent judge, philosopher and mentor who said not a word, but still showed the way. A gentle voice from within seemed to say, "Ameeta, time and tide wait for no man. Opportunity is miserly in dishing out chances, so grab it now or it may be too late."

Her mind flashed back to the day she was barely twenty two. The appointment letter in her hand was to be her passport to the professional world. She remembered how stunning she had looked in a sari, (the traditional six-yard garment worn by Indian women)on the day of her interview. Soon after she got her masters' from the Institute for World Class Leaders, she had applied for an assistant professor's post there. Her confidence had been high as she faced the interview,because she had known she could walk into a job of her choice with the resumé she had had. The management had not advertised for this post, as they had felt their students should be encouraged to join the institute. As expected, the job was hers and she was thrilled, but a bit apprehensive about rubbing shoulders with those who had taught her till very recently. She even dreamt of how the students would jeer at her in her first lecture and give terrible feedback about her. Mercifully, nothing like that had happened.

She clearly remembered pressing the elevator button meant only for the staff, and handing over her papers to the Deputy Director, Dr. Sasi Kumar. He shook hands with her and said, "Welcome! Congratulations." He had then given her some good-natured advice. As she came out of the cabin she had bumped into Gautam Kapoor, one year her senior, who was then teaching there. He had said, "Great to have you around among the old crones. They are okay, but I can very well do with some young company."

Over the months, Ameeta had grown in popularity with her students and the management had been happy with her too. On the personal front, Gautam and she had been going steady and had planned their wedding in the following year, around January. They had enjoyed clandestine meetings during their courtship and had been like love birds who could not live without each other.

It was not funny when they had run into her parents' friends at a movie hall once. They were curious to know from her, who Gautam was? She had enjoyed playing the avoiding game. At times, she had felt one of those people should go and spill the beans to her parents, and then the cat would be out of the bag and her job would be easier. But Gautam, the cautious one, had made sure nothing like that had happened, because he believed in directly approaching the two families. Ameeta had not agreed with Gautam, but then she had been madly in love with him, so she had gone his way.

One day, Mrs. Kaul had bumped into Ameeta and Gautam in a restaurant. Before Ameeta could say a word to answer the lady's probing eyes, Gautam had excused himself and gone out. Poor Ameeta had had to make lame excuses about how her group was waiting for them outside and how she was getting late. She also knew the lady was far from convinced by her excuses and would be the proverbial Good Samaritan she had been hoping for. Ameeta wanted her mother's close buddy to act in character as the conscience keeper of society and be the tell-tale. Mrs. Kaul's daughter Minni had eloped with their young driver and the family had never heard the end of it. But strange is the behaviour of these socialites! They think it is their bounden duty to save the youth and their parents from the irreparable damage being done. The poor parents, according to them, become the laughing stock of society, and must be kept informed.

But for some unknown reason, Mrs. Kaul had not told her friends and Ameeta's mother about Gautam. Ameeta had thought, "Unlikely to be a lapse of memory though! More likely she is waiting for the golden moment to strike." Sadly, that moment had never come.

 The reason was, Gautam, for some time, had been pushing that both of them tell their respective parents. So, with her heart in her mouth, one Saturday, Ameeta had brought up the subject of Gautam and herself. There had been, (as expected in a highly traditional upper middle class Indian family), total opposition. Fireworks, and then pin drop silence had followed for days on end. Ameeta had preferred it when all hell was let lose. Then she could vocally support Gautam's cause. Instead, her father had gone into a shell. It was self-imposed silence and his way of punishing her.

On the other hand, her mother had openly cursed her fate and bemoaned the day Ameeta had taken up the teaching job after her masters in management. That, she felt was the root cause. Mr. Gautam would have been nowhere on the horizon. She was convinced he was nothing but a gold digger. She had been so proud of the alliances that had been pouring in for her daughter from enviable business families, senior government officials and politicians. Ameeta could be the favoured daughter-in-law with her credentials. But all this cut no ice with her pigheaded daughter whose resolve to marry Gautam became even stronger. Every time her mother had called him a cur, or unscrupulous, she had sung odes of praise of him.

Ameeta's mother, Mrs. Ranjan Lal became the butt of false sympathy at cards and coffee parties and people invariably laughed behind her back saying, "So the great one has come down to earth from the clouds. Her arrogance has taken a beating." Some mean friends told her to her face, to be warned against a wife beater for a son-in-law, who could drive Ameeta to hanging herself from the ceiling.

Ameeta had decided she was the master of her own destiny and would marry Gautam. She would lie on the bed she had chosen, be it full of roses or thorns. Who was to stop her? The impasse was broken by Ameeta's mother. Realising that her daughter would not give in, she had cajoled her sulking husband to visit Gautam's parents and take the next step before Ameeta could resort to any extreme step. He reluctantly agreed to go over to the Kapoors' residence on the outskirts of Mumbai. Of course, Ameeta was on cloud nine at her success. It was a gleeful victory. When her parents left, like a cat who had lapped up a bowl of cream,she had laid on her bed reading Business India. She had barely turned the first page when she had gone into a reverie about Gautam, justifying all his minus points and thinking about her future with her dream man.

Suddenly, the doorbell had rung and their domestic help had opened it. Her parents had returned in less than twenty minutes as if they had returned from a funeral. Her father had looked through her and gone into the study. Her mother had told her that her father had stopped the car to the side of the road, and told her that he couldn't go through all this insult. He had then started the ignition saying, "Even for Ameeta, I can't go through with this torture. After all, I am the president of a blue-chip company. What is Gautam's father? A mere non-entity! Barely became a senior assistant in a small bottle-making company!"

Just as her mother had been telling her this, her father had come out of the study and said, "Ameeta, you have decided to marry a riff-raff who can barely boast of some education within the country. If he were from the Ivy League colleges, I could have consoled myself that with the right education, status and money would follow. The academic credentials would have been a consolation."

He had gone on to say that he would break rather than bend. "What can the Kapoor family offer you? What you get as pocket money, they can barely spend in a month," he had smirked, and had pursued further to question, "What can they offer you, my girl? You will languish in a middle-class family or come away before the month is over."

He had said aloud to no one in particular, "Who has made this weird custom of the girl's father bending backwards to say, 'Please accept the hand of my daughter for your son.'I can't do all this Ameeta, not even for you. I foresee the future where you are a doormat or the proverbial lamb to the slaughter."

Ameeta had not been moved by this speech and Mrs. Ranjan Lal had thought her husband was an egoist. Any girl's father had to follow traditions to see the girl get married. She remembered her father, a rich aristocrat going to her in-laws' house and following the protocol even though their family had not been a patch on her own."That is, after all, the done thing in India and my pompous husband will have to do it sooner or later," she had thought.

She had said loud and clear, "When Ameeta was born, you should have realised and prepared yourself for what it takes to see a girl married! Don't you realise that you are not the first or the last father of a daughter in this world?" Mr. Ranjan Lal had glared at his wife in reply and had walked out of the house in a huff.

Ameeta had been unable to understand all the fuss her father was making. So she put more pressure on her mother to get her Dad and his inflated ego to come around.

Soon, about a month later, both the families had met in a restaurant. Gautam's family had been no happier than Ranjan Lal's family but had gone ahead for their son's sake. Both the fathers had agreed that they were not in favour of the children's decision to marry and it was being thrust on them. Mr. Kapoor had said, "Anyway, we have no choice so let us get them married before they say a child is on the way. Or is it the case already Mr. Ranjan Lal? Are my dumb son and your daughter living together?"

Mr. Ranjan Lal had looked the colour of ripe tomatoes and wanted to teach that man a lesson. But he had kept quiet because this angle had not struck him. He had had no defence for his daughter's conduct or preference for Gautam. Instead,he had been even more convinced than earlier that Gautam had masterminded everything. But his inner voice had said, "Do you think your daughter is such a weakling to meekly go by his plans? No way!"

The wedding had been fixed for the 20th of July. The only two who rejoiced had been Gautam and Ameeta. Mr. Kapoor, after the meeting in the restaurant,had been sure his stupid son had chosen a girl from a very affluent family, far above their strata and would pay a heavy price. It was just a question of time before the girl would throw her weight around and flaunt her parental wealth. Gautam would be no better than a puppy in his in-laws' house, he felt. He was sorry for his wife, Sarla. She was a mild, soft-spoken person and Ameeta was going to walk all over her! He had felt that there were undoubtedly dark clouds ahead and they had gone wrong in the parenting of their son or they wouldn't have been subjected to all that. His thoughts had concluded with the age-old saying,'No use crying over spilt milk."'

The wedding had been a fairly grand one. Not because of the joy a daughter's wedding usually brings, but because Mr. Ranjan Lal had a position to maintain in society. He could not publicly voice his dislike or disdain for Gautam. All his hopes of having a highly eligible son-in-law had been dashed and he was doing only what was expected of him so that no eyebrows were raised. He had had a plastic smile right through the wedding and he had clearly ignored Gautam's side of the family and this had not gone unnoticed by the guests. Some of them had even whispered, "Poor Ranjan Lal has had to swallow a bitter pill!"

Ameeta's father had always had nightmares about his daughter getting married and leaving for her new home and much more about the actual day of her departure with all the misgivings he had. He had visualised his daughter taking puffed rice and throwing it behind her. (It is a way of saying good bye to the parental home, the end of one era and the beginning of another.) He had seen the movie,'Father of the Bride' a number of times during the course of the wedding preparations and had cried unashamedly at the thought of the impending ceremonies and his worst fears coming true. The newly-weds had been in their own blissful world, unaware of the grief they had caused their parents.

When the couple had returned to work after the honeymoon, (which they had gone on, through the kind courtesy of Mr. Ranjan Lal), they had lived with the senior Kapoors. The romance had been enough for Ameeta to not worry about living with her in-laws. It had suited her fine, as she had no responsibilities in the kitchen, or rather ignored them, and both, Gautam and she went to college together, went over to her parents after work, and came home to sleep or sometimes for dinner. Gautam had surprisingly adapted to the lifestyle of his in-laws that included going to clubs, drinking and eating in five-star hotels. So the father-in law, Mr. Ranjan Lal had begun to tolerate Gautam for being street smart and cultivating all the tastes and style that go with the rich. The old man had said among his friends, "Thank God! Gautam knows what is good for him. With this attitude, he will go places." The friends in turn had thought that it was a case of 'New brooms sweep well'.

On the other side of the fence, Mr. Kapoor had been miserable with the turn of events though it was not unexpected. His son was fast losing his self-respect. Mr. Kapoor sure he would soon come to grief. He had no time for his family and what was worse, he was aping the rich rather than helping his family financially. He was a mere hen-pecked husband and Ameeta was the daughter of a rich man and not their daughter-in-law. She almost never stepped into the kitchen and wanted to be waited upon like a queen. She was living like a guest but Sarla never complained and had been willing to give her rich daughter-in-law some more time to take on her responsibilities.

Seema, Gautam's sister had come down from Calcutta to her parents' home for her first delivery, a good eight months after Gautam's wedding. The day their granddaughter had come into the world, Ameeta's mother-in-law had asked her to sleep over at the hospital. Gautam had been listening to this conversation from the next room. Ameeta had replied politely but firmly, "Maji(mother-in-law), my family wants Gautam and me to meet some important friends who have come down from the USA. There is the hospital staff and in addition, you can hire a private ayah(maid servant) if you can't cope. In any case, I am not a maid in the family. If it helps, I will ask my mother's domestic help to come over. You can pay her something." Mr. Kapoor had said, "Sarla, don't bother to ask. I can sleep outside the room and help out. Have you forgotten that our son is Gautam Lal and not a Kapoor any longer?"

Ameeta had ignored her father-in-law's comments.

But that night, Gautam had been really mad at Ameeta and his foul mood had led to their first big fight. He had not raised his voice but had conveyed his displeasure. He had said that he had gone out of the way to accommodate her and her family and she, on the other hand, could not sacrifice one evening for his family. They had hurled abuses at each other and it had ended in Ameeta crying and Gautam being silent. Gautam, thinking later in a cooler frame of mind, had decided that such fights are a part of a marriage and he should woo back his lady love. This was the pattern always, and Ameeta had never once apologised. Over the weekend, Ameeta's parents had came over to see the baby and gave expensive gifts to Seema and her child. The Kapoors had not wanted a showdown, so they accepted them.

Around this time when Seema was with them, Ameeta had begun complaining that the flat was cramped and Gautam and she should move out to live on their own or move to her parents' home. Gautam had been reluctant to make this move till he got a better job. But that very morning, instead of going to college for work Ameeta had gone to her parents to ask them to bail her out by giving her the deposit money for leasing an apartment. The parents had been only too glad to help out their daughter. Her mother had praised her for adjusting so well in her in-laws family. Only the Kapoors could have told them the real story. Ameeta's mother had been glad that now she could boast of her daughter's address being Bandra and not Navi Mumbai.

Having got her way, Ameeta had been in a very good mood. The next day when she went to the college staff room she got chatting with Satinder Singh, a visiting faculty. He was a tall, handsome man who worked for a multinational company. She had noticed the disarming smile, athletic body and fun-loving disposition. He had looked at her and asked sympathetically as to why she was not herself those days. He had asked if it was due to problems with her new husband.

"Nothing serious," she had replied without looking up. Suddenly, she had looked up and asked if he knew of any places for rent in downtown Mumbai. He had smiled and asked her to give him a day's time to come up with something.

Sure enough, the next day he had had good news for her. She had thought of how resourceful he was! The apartment was a spacious two bedroom, one overlooking the sea. It was in the same block as Satinder's flat at Worli sea-face, a fairly elite address. She had gone over to her parents to collect the cheque for the deposit. This was the first time that Gautam had not accompanied her to his in-laws' place. She had been elated and for the first time, had felt that her in-laws lacked class and she had been somewhat ashamed of their lifestyle. Gautam, on the other hand, had been disgusted with Ameeta's way of asking for and getting things from her parents. What she was trying to prove he did not know! The cheque signed by his father-in-law had upset him no end. He would have looked for a place once he had known the outcome of his job interview. But as usual, he had lost the argument to Ameeta and they had shifted over the weekend, with Satinder playing the part of Man Friday to perfection. For some unknown reason, Satinder had irked Gautam. The only silver lining had been that Gautam had got the job of deputy director in a prestigious teaching institute.

Ameeta had gradually but definitely found a marked change in Gautam's attitude. He was unwilling to go over to his in-laws' and she had had to constantly make excuses for his absence to her family and their friends. She would dump a sulking Gautam and go with her friends for movies. All this had certainly raised eyebrows. Her parents had not been blind to the changes but had chosen not to intervene. Ameeta had refused to visit her in-laws. All this had resulted in Gautam spending more time alone and the ashtray piling up with cigarette butts faster than one would have liked to see.

During their frequent fights, Ameeta would ask Gautam, "What has come over you? Why have you changed so much?" She would attempt to make truce by bargaining, "I will come to your parents only if you come to mine." Normally,Gautam would be silent to her questions, but at times he would say, "I tried to change during the courtship and in the initial stage of our marriage to please you. But it did not help me. My self-esteem is very important and that was taking a beating." On a rare occasion, he would say how slighted his parents had felt at the attitude of her parents and her attitude in particular. He too had some pride. Of course, Ameeta would say that she had married him and not his family. Their middle-class values had bugged her no end. Once during an argument it had struck her that she may tire of Gautam. Quickly, she had brushed the thought aside and had said to herself that all this was a passing phase.

Gradually, Ameeta was more in Sati's company and unconsciously, had begun to ignore her beloved Gautam. The former had empathised with her but never belittled Gautam. He had felt sorry for Gautam for marrying a girl far above his status. He should have known what he was getting into when he had tied the knot. But he could not blame him either, for Ameeta was both smart and beautiful. Gautam had not realised he would have to contend with a totally spoilt brat of a daughter and wife.

Gautam had bought a used car thinking he could please his wife. The thorn in his flesh was Sati who was a very suave and rich guy who was luring Ameeta away from him. He would stay over at their place for late night coffees or pay the bill at expensive restaurants. The three of them went to eat out often. Ameeta had not seemed too impressed by the car but used it to go to work and to get around. So the net result was that the car was never available for Gautam's parents even in an emergency. So, one more effort at pleasing his wife and her parents had failed.

One day in a huff, she said that she was going to ask her parents for a new car for her coming birthday. "What is the harm?" she had thought, and rationalized, "they are my parents after all! If they can help, and want to, why can't I ask them? I don't find it wrong." She had repeated this to Sati on the phone and Gautam had been pained to overhear it. He had felt guilty that his parents had been struggling and did not complain. Their eyes spoke more than anything else and were like barbs at each other. The truth had dawned on him that he would have to lie on the bed he had made. It served him right. If his parents had grumbled or taunted him, he would have felt better and less remorseful.

For Sati, the compulsive flirt that he was, Ameeta was one more conquest which his affluence made possible. He was smart enough not to force the pace of his romance but felt she should chuck Gautam and then he could get her a good job and set her up. She deserved that. She, he noticed, was totally pampered and bratty. She had mistaken infatuation for love. She sure was a nit-wit!

Often, Gautam had pondered and looked out for ways by which Ameeta and his parents could be brought together. One day, like Archimedes, he had come up with a brain-wave. He had thought of having a child, as the ideal solution to make them bond. He had coaxed Ameeta into a holiday at a nearby hill-station. It had been a disaster and on their return, it was like jumping from the frying pan into the fire. On their return, his in-laws had been waiting at the door. They wanted to ask their daughter what colour car she would prefer. Gautam realised that night that Ameeta was more their daughter and Sati's buddy and less his wife, for she was carried away by glamour and luxuries. She was not willing to wait for anything. He had felt that he was reduced to an appendage in her and her parents' life. But still, he had felt that all was not lost and miracles did happen. Something would change his wife, Ameeta!

By a strange quirk of fate, Ameeta had become pregnant. Panic had gripped her and she had argued with the doctor, who had known her since her birth, that it was impossible, for she had never been off the pill. The doctor had nodded and said that the test was positive and had congratulated her and had said with a wink, "Mistakes do happen with newlyweds. Your parents will be on cloud nine when you break the news to them."

But Ameeta had cried all the way home. When she was calmer at home, she had decided that neither her parents nor Gautam should know, or she would be trapped and doomed. She had said aloud, "I should have an abortion. Sati, maybe, can help me." Her first reaction had been, "Oh no! What did I say? It amounts to murder!" In the next breath she had thought, "Mistakes have to be rectified, so what is wrong? I have the right to have the baby when I want and with whom I want." The next second she was thinking, "Oh no! Have I lost my mind to say all this or is my marriage already over that I said 'whom I want'?" She had made herself a cup of coffee to settle her nerves. She had thought, "I do love Gautam but how did such a costly mistake occur? Maybe in the hotel that night, I forgot to take the pill."

"Too bad," she had concluded. "We humans make mistakes. To err is human and to love divine." "Really?" asked a sarcastic inner voice. "Don't delude yourself."

At work the next morning, Sati had been there before her. As she had walked in, he had smiled at her and said, "Hi Ami, I have great news for you! Let's meet at the cafeteria for coffee and chat all about it during the break." She had not missed out on his familiarity in addressing her. He had told her over coffee that there was a job opening in his company for heading a key project. "Send your resumé and leave the rest to me." Of course, she had been elated with the news and had thought,"Sati is a real go-getter. Gautam is incapable of such actions as he is cocooned in his comfort zone."

She had remembered the baby and had felt a bit bad for a second, but then decided that with this opportunity, there was no way she could go ahead with the pregnancy. By the end of the week, the job was hers, but she had certainly known that she had not got it on her merit. Gautam would certainly not like the turn of events as she would have to travel a bit.

Gautam had tried to be happy about the job for Ameeta's sake and had treated her at a new place that had opened close by. There, she had told him what a brick Sati had been in getting her the job. That had spoilt it for Gautam because he had thought, "Why should this guy take over our lives all the time?"

He had been disappointed that Ameeta had got the job through Sati's recommendation and not her own abilities. He had wondered why Ameeta's work ethics were changing. This meant that she was drifting away from him. Not fair at all!

The celebration had been on a Saturday evening and Sati had fixed up an appointment for Ameeta with Dr. Sweta on Monday. Ameeta had had to seek Sati's help as she had not wanted to divulge the problem to her friends. Gautam's help had been out of the question. She had been more than surprised that Sati had solutions to every problem. She had wondered, "How does he know a gynaecologist? Has he got other girls into trouble earlier? Why am I being such a nosey parker by wanting to know about his life so much?" she had chided herself.

On Sunday, she had wanted to call the doctor to clear some doubts before seeing her, so she had called her when Gautam was in the bath. It was safe. Unfortunately, just then Gautam had come out to pick a clean towel and had heard everything. He had been so angry that he had pulled the phone from her and demanded an explanation. He had said that she had crossed all limits of decency by not telling him this very important news. He was after all the father and had every right to know and she must continue with the pregnancy. It meant so much to so many people.

Ameeta's tone had not been as aggressive as it had been on earlier occasions, but had been firm when she said the timing was wrong and Gautam had no right to spoil her chances. They had all their lives ahead to have a child. It was not the end of the world. Gautam's pleading had cut no ice and the next day she had gone ahead with her plan and met the doctor.

Gautam had realised that contrary to popular belief, women were not soft and sensitive, but cruel. He had shed a tear at the thought of the life which would die even before entering the world. He had decided to help Ameeta with her decision, but she had refused saying, "Why this kindness now? You have never been a supportive husband when moving out of the in-laws' house or getting the new car. You are being most unreasonable."

Now Gautam had begun to have doubts about Ameeta's loyalty and was really in the dumps. He hated doubting his wife and felt that he should work harder to make the marriage work. He could go abroad and get away from his in-laws, Sati and this city which had once promised so much, but offered nothing but misery now. The idea had brought him some cheer but it was short-lived as the following Saturday, he had found the main door open and Ameeta had come in looking pale, and leaning on Sati's shoulder. She lay on the couch and Sati too had made himself comfortable on the couch as if there was nothing for the three of them to worry about. He had mentioned in passing that he was going to Delhi to attend the golden jubilee celebration of his family business started by his grandfather. He had advised Gautam that Ameeta could do with some rest. Gautam and she could think of a vacation. They were free to use his family's company guest house five hours away on the coast. Ameeta had thanked Sati for the offer but later had told Gautam that he better not come as he would make her morose with his lecturing and middle-class values. She had wanted to be alone.

He had seen off Ameeta the next morning and had asked her to call once she reached the guest house and give him the contact numbers too.

He had come in to an empty house and had felt hollow and cheated in every way. The idea of a divorce had come to him time and again that morning and he had thought he would open up to his father what he had bottled up for so long and seek his advice. In a day or two, before Ameeta returned on Wednesday, he would do that. Maybe his father would help Ameeta see some sense and that would give a genuine chance to this relationship founded on love. Just as he was leaving for work on Monday, he got a call from his uncle saying that his father had had a fall in the bathroom and had died immediately.

Gautam could not believe the news. He changed into a white kurta-pyjama and left for his parents' house. All the way he was wondering what excuse he would make for Ameeta's absence and was livid with her for putting him in this predicament. As he parked the car he saw a fairly large crowd in front of their ground floor flat. He had been trying to figure out his family's thoughts - about the irresponsible son he undoubtedly was and the henpecked husband who had deserted his parents. "Can I blame them?" he had thought, "Particularly when I have come here alone at this critical time."

On seeing his mother he had been terribly moved and had cried unashamedly. Some of the women had asked him where the daughter-in-law was. He heard himself saying impersonally, "She was sent on some official work and will come back once she gets the message."

"Liar," said an inner voice, "How can you lie at such a time? You have lost your wife first and now your father without even a goodbye though you are in the same city. Shame on you! You have been a bad son and a worse husband. You have pleased none."

His in-laws had come in looking appropriately grief-stricken, fake or otherwise but asked him a couple of times why Ameeta was not there. They had definitely been more worried about what people would make of her absence. His father-in-law had offered to go down and bring her himself as the occasion was one where no excuses were enough. Then Gautam had told him why Ameeta couldn't be there for the funeral and that his sister would arrive once the flight came in.

As he had stood in front of the pyre, he had felt miserable and had kept saying, "Sorry Dad, for being a bad son and causing you so much anguish. Just when I needed to talk, you chose to abandon me. I deserve it." He did not hear the priest but acted mechanically.

Gautam had returned on the next day to his flat to see if Ameeta was back and to take her to his mother. She was not there and he had been sure the message he had sent her had reached her. In any case, she should be back latest by the next morning. He was not sure what Ameeta wanted from life but for him, a divorce was unthinkable in the changed scenario as he could not afford to pay any alimony. His mother was a silent sufferer and he understood her many doubts and insecurities at that juncture. At least now, he had felt she needed his shoulder in every way and he must give it, but would Ameeta allow it was the question that had haunted him. Would Ameeta relent and allow his mother to stay with them, was the million dollar question.

At the guest house called Lover's Abode, Sati had come to see if Ameeta and Gautam were comfortable. On seeing her alone he had thought the heavens were really playing up and he had stayed to have lunch before he left for Delhi. He had told her all about his family and how she could be the perfect daughter-in-law. He had said that he had told them about her and his intentions. Initially, there had been resistance to her being married and seeking a divorce. But emotional blackmail had helped as he was their only son and heir to the business. Now his parents were fine with it,though they would have preferred an unmarried girl from the same business and religious community.

Ameeta had listened to all this with her mouth open, totally dumbstruck. At last she had said, "Sati, give me a break. I need time to think. It's all so sudden." Sati had said with a flourish, "Take all the time, my love, but say yes. I will make up for all that you have missed out with Gautam." He had given her a peck and said,"I will see you on my return from Delhi."

Ameeta got back to her room and had felt somewhat dizzy after all that had transpired. She had felt that Sati had taken over her life and made all the decisions and that she was meekly toeing the line. Was there a catch in all that Sati was offering? Was he a real smooth operator? She had realised for the first time that she had not once missed Gautam but for a minute, her heart did beat a bit faster when she thought of the peck Sati had given her. She was afraid to accept the truth that Gautam was her past. But what she did not know was, if Sati should be her future.

On her return, she had driven to her parents' place and not her apartment because she had not been yet ready to face Gautam after the events in the guest house. To her surprise, she had not found her parents at home and the cleaning woman opened the door and told her that they were with Gautam because his father had died on Monday morning. Her first reaction had been that she was in no mood to give him her shoulder to cry on for she had tolerated his folks for his sake. Surprisingly, she had felt no regret about her abortion. As she lay on her familiar bed, she had told herself that decisions were to be taken as per the situation prevailing at the time, so why regret anything.

The Lals had been with Gautam and had voiced their concern about Ameeta's absence and suggested that he come over to them instead of being alone. He had politely refused and had said his family needed him at that time, so he would be there. Mr. Ranjan Lal had agreed and said that both Ameeta and he should help the family get on its feet again and make the necessary changes. Mrs. Ranjan Lal had been very unhappy with Ameeta's attitude as she had had to bear catty comments from the womenfolk who even went to the extent of saying that rich, working daughters-in-law were no good. It had been meant for her ears.

When they returned, the phone had been ringing. Ranjan Lal had picked it up and had been surprised to hear one Mr. Satinder Singh asking if Ameeta was available and if she was feeling okay. Ranjan Lal had replied that he had just come back and had no idea that his daughter was sick, as she was supposed to be at some training programme. When he had asked who the caller was and how he knew his daughter,the phone was disconnected. The reply was stone-deaf silence. "Strange, very strange," thought Ranjan Lal. Ameeta had come down when she heard the phone ring. She had heard her father's side of the conversation and guessed that it was Sati. "How he cares!" she had thought.

Her parents had shared the news of the events of the time she had been away and had told her that now she should make amends by standing by her bereaved family. Ameeta had made some lame excuse and that had got Ranjan Lal thinking about the phone call and his daughter's almost inhuman reaction. He had sensed that something messy was in the air. But he hadn't been able to figure out what it was, more because of his love for his daughter.

A few minutes later, Ameeta had gone to her office, and later to the beach, to let her thoughts crystallize.

Mrs. Ranjan Lal had thought that her daughter had gone to her in-laws. She had sighed with relief.

Ameeta realised she was at the cross-roads of life and she depended on Mother Nature to show her the way, as always. She felt bad that she had thought so little about her guiding force after her wedding and was glad to be back. The only doubt that bothered her about Sati was how his attitude towards her would be once they were married? What if she was made to feel inferior because she was not as rich as his family? Would she be able to handle her life and his people or would he turn out to be another Gautam?

She questioned and satisfied her conscience that not everyone was bad. But how would her parents take it? Was the divorce fair? "Well," she thought, "Is a life of drudgery fair on me? Yes, my parents had warned me, but if I made a mistake I have to correct it and I have a golden opportunity with Sati. Not everyone is so lucky. The most important question is, will Gautam let me off easily and agree to the divorce?" She said to herself, "One thing at a time, Ameeta. Take it easy. Remember to never look back but look ahead. Irrespective of Sati, leave Gautam, as he is no good for you."

When she went home, she sat next to her father. Mercifully, her mother was in the kitchen so she blurted out, "Dad, I want a divorce. It's over between Gautam and me. I tried, but it did not work." Her mother walked in just then. Both parents said, "That's impossible!" After her parents' tirade ended, she only said, "Dad, I have decided not to go back to Gautam. We are incompatible and if you don't want me home, I will move out on my own. You saying, 'I told you so' will be no good."

To make sure his precious daughter was not wrecking her life once again, her father took her out for dinner and quizzed her. After some persuasion, she came out with the whole story about Gautam and her, and how she had survived by taking unilateral decisions even though they hurt Gautam no end. After all, till then she had had everything for the asking, so she had thought why not Gautam; but now it was all over. Her father asked her if there was someone else on the scene. She could not avoid the direct question and told him everything about Sati. He nodded his head and said, "A known devil is better than an unknown angel. So patch up darling, for it may be from the frying pan into the fire."

She responded, "It is worth trying the unknown angel for whatever it is worth." While he paid the bill he said aloud, "Why did we spoil you so much that you have landed in this situation today! Your stubborn ways could prove very costly." She smiled and said, "Thanks Dad, for everything. We will see who is right, you or I. The first round you won, but the second I am sure I will."

On her father's advice, Ameeta waited for the thirteen days of mourning to pass. Then she made two calls. The first, to Gautam whom she had loved dearly once and fought the world to marry, and the other, to the man she believed she loved now. When Gautam picked up the phone she said, "Goodbye Gautam. I'm sorry it ended this way. Once, I really did love you but I did not realise we are from two different worlds. You were and are a gentleman, so please do make it mutual."

Gautam was silent for a minute, for he had lost all, so what was there to fight for? He said in that second, most gently, "Send the papers and you will be Ameeta Ranjan Lal once again. I guess I have to thank Sati for this hell I am going through."

"Yes," she replied honestly and he ended with, "I hope he does what I failed to do for you."

Ameeta was all excited at the next call as things had worked so easily for her. She called Sati and said, "Let's celebrate my freedom and our engagement. It is a big YES from me!"

Sati said, "What engagement and whom are you talking about?"

"Ours, yours and mine, my darling," she cooed into the phone.

"You got it all wrong," he replied and said that he would be insane to get married to a divorcee from an upper middle-class family when there were millions of unmarried girls from the rich upper-class dying to marry him…

"Don't joke with me. It is no laughing matter. You said your parents had given their blessings. So come down and meet my parents."

The last sentence Sati said before Ameeta cut him off was, "Oh! Did I tell you that? I said it to get you out of the dumps and it was nothing serious. You should have valued your kind Gautam a little more."

As she banged the receiver down, Ameeta's knees wobbled and she sat on the sofa. Her father had heard it all on the other instrument and came rushing down. He held his daughter as if she were seven-years-old and said, "I am with you through thick and thin, my little one. Yes, it is a harsh world where the middle-class are boring constants and the very rich, spoilt children make mistakes and their parents hold their hands at such times. But we are parents till our last breath."

When years later Ameeta remarried and became a mother, she remembered her father's wise words.

AN EVENING IN KINNAR: POLITICAL AWAKENING!

It was Friday, the thirteenth of October and people were celebrating Dushera. In North India, people believe in Lord Rama, who epitomises good and had vanquished and killed the demon king, Ravan on this day. In the South, the significance and beliefs are different. The all-powerful Maa Kaali had killed the demon Mahishasura and the South Indians celebrate the victory as Vijayadashmi. In some other parts of the country, it is the day when the five Pandava brothers came out of their exile, picked up their weapons and fought the Mahabharata war at Kurukshetra. Whatever be the reason, Rama, Kaali or Krishna, Hindu's rejoice and celebrate the triumph of good over evil. This is in keeping with the Hindu Vedic philosophy that God comes down to earth in every age when evil prevails over good. He shows that the path of divinity is supreme and that He will fight to establish the power of good over evil.

Each and every family in the small town of Kinnar in Karnataka had decorated their house, small or big, with strings of brightly-coloured marigolds and fresh mango leaves which hung artistically from their main doors. The entrances of the houses were beautified with intricate designs filled with red, green, white, dark blue, orange and purple coloured Rangoli, locally called Muggu.

The women and teenage girls allowed their creative juices to flow, as their delicate fingers moved deftly to the many melodious folk songs sung by the older generation to entertain everyone around.

The middle-aged women busied themselves cooking many goodies like the mouth-watering South Indian delicacy Bobbattu known as Pooranpoli in Maharashtra. The main course was lemon rice or coconut rice with a curry with gravy or stew. Most of the ingredients used were what was locally available from the fields or dairy products from the cows and buffaloes they kept in the backyard. They used milk, rice, coconut, jaggery and sesame seeds. Kids stealthily tasted the mouth-watering goodies. Sometimes, the older boys sent the innocent young children to steal the goodies for them. They hoped the little ones would have their ears boxed if caught stealing. They could slink away while the younger kids got the royal balking.

The vibrant-coloured long skirts and blouses, or the half-sari and the regular six yards sari completed the festive look of fun and frolic. People forgot their differences big or small and reinforced their faith in friendship and goodwill by hugging each other, exchanging greetings, gifts and sweets. They all wanted peace and goodwill to prevail.

That year, Kinnar was excited for another reason too. The local elections for the state assembly were announced for the 14th of October. The announcements and jingles on the radio and television added to the auspicious beginning. As is customary, the Election Day would be a holiday for offices, schools and the one college they had. Those buildings would be used as polling stations for the elections. The campaigning would end today and then the hopefuls would wait anxiously for the electorate to cast their precious vote. Their next five years depended on tomorrow. The student community was the happiest as they got an additional holiday.

Voting Day is the one time in every five years, when the voter feels like a monarch. The common man has the power to bring a party to power or dump it. Party workers and leaders woo voters in royal style similar to how the bridegroom and his family are treated on the wedding day. Friend and foe alike greeted voters and coaxed them to vote for their party or candidate. Handbills were pushed into the voters' hands with a smile and sweets were distributed. Personal invitations for the public meeting in the temple courtyard today were extended. Shrewd politicians knew the platform suitable to woo the voters and today could not have been a better time. The mood of the public was perfect. The venue was excellent as everyone wanted to seek the blessings of the Gram-devata, the reigning deity of the village. The attendance would be near hundred percent.

After a hearty festive meal, people began to move towards the temple located on the right bank of river Krishna. The events that made history or created milestones in the lives of the locals were all held in the extensive temple courtyard.

As mentioned, today the attraction of visiting the temple was twofold, religious and political. Hardly anyone stayed home for their accustomed afternoon siesta. Even thieves gave up their livelihood for a while, though the timing was perfect for a bit of loot. They arrived like gentlemen in clean clothes. It was their way of paying their respects to the Goddess.

The idol of Maa Kaali in black granite was revered because they wholeheartedly believed that she bestows boons on her deserving devotees and also punishes the guilty. Her eyes emit fire and her tongue hangs out in fury. One of her four hands holds the head of a demon. Her hair loose up to the waist appears to be flying. For all her children, she is the divine Shakti, which is omnipresent in Prakriti (nature)in manifold forms.

In the background, the beating of drums alternated with the auspicious Nadaswaram, heralding the all-important occasion. From the eastern and western entrance of the temple, women and men were seen walking hand in hand smiling and exchanging festive greetings with a hug. Behind them, two bulls walked from each of the entrances towards the central court of the temple. The smooth temple floor was spic and span. The pillars were decorated with bright-coloured flower garlands, loosely wound round them. The central entrance was decorated with strings of white jasmines hanging like a curtain.

The two bulls were deep dark brown in colour, almost merging into black. The sheen of their coats showed their pedigree and their healthy bodies. Their eyes shone and the bells in their necks jingled to the rhythm of their walk, which was a trifle quick. They wore blood-red rose garlands around their necks. The atmosphere was charged with unbelievable excitement and high expectations.

From the eastern entrance,Buddhi,(meaning intellect) made his entrance. He was followed by the local candidates, important personalities and party workers of the 'People's Progress Party'. The leader, Guru, a man in his thirties, was patting Buddhi to calm him because animals are sensitive to loud sounds. Guru, a visionary, had an outstanding academic record, with a master's degree in Political Science from the University of Bombay. Soon after leaving the university, he plunged headlong into an active political career. He held the conviction that he could guide his people to move towards self-development and prosperity, while adhering strictly to the best principles of democracy. He removed his footwear in front of the main entrance of the temple, closed his eyes, folded his hands in all humility and bowed his head before Maa Kaali and then moved to a seat, which had seen better days.

From the western side came the other bull, Balwan (meaning brawn), that turned its garlanded head to the words,"*Balwan ye pehalwan hamaara, pehalwan ki jai*". A foreigner in the crowds asked a neighbour who spoke English what that one liner meant. Promptly came the reply in broken English, "The big bull, Balwan is strong like a wrestler. Victory to him."Balwan shook his head rather vigorously and walked like a peacock, oozing arrogance.

Durga Das, popularly known by one and all as 'Dada', followed the animal. Few remembered his formal name. 'Dada', a self-styled leader was orphaned before he could crawl. As a result, formal education was out of the question for him. Life was his 'teacher'. He followed the law of the jungle and indulged in anti-social activities. His self-esteem was sky-high. He was always dressed in white. Today it was spotless white, washed by the local dhobi (washerman) who was almost never paid. Dada's beard was untrimmed and his wavy hair, rather long. He was chewing tobacco and waving to anyone who acknowledged him.

A small crowd gathered around him. He talked to them and patted a few backs but from the corner of his eyes, he slyly looked at Tanushree, the only child of Raju, the wealthy zamindar (land owner). As her name suggested, she was undoubtedly endowed with rare beauty and grace. She was unaware of her stunning looks and the surreptitious glances from Dada as she laughed and joked with her friends. Tanushree had brains too and was very well-educated. Dada, in his heart of hearts admired educated people but ran down education in public. He hoped to marry Tanushree by hook or crook once he won the election.

Dada spotted Guru and swaggered up to him, hugged him ostentatiously and said, "I bring greetings today from my party to you and your party." Guru reciprocated his party's greetings of peace and goodwill. The drums stopped beating and the priest said in his clear, gentle voice, which echoed through the loud speakers,"Victory to you all. May the Divine Mother bless each one of you present here. This year's annual bullfight is to humour us all and maybe forecast the political future for Kinnar. Buddhi and Balwan will participate in the fight. As is customary, the head of the vanquished bull will be offered to Maa Kaali, who alone knows what is best for us, her children."

Even today in the twenty-first century, we can't totally give up being superstitious. People felt that Maa Kaali was guiding them and they ought to vote for the party whose bull won that day.

Dada, as usual, keen to have the last word took the mike and said, "My party believes we are with the people and they need me to think for the good of my people living here. I am pleased to be honoured this way by Maa Herself. Kinnar is Dada and your Dada is Kinnar."

Quickly the drums began to beat to a crescendo and then Guru and Dada walked up to the two heroes of the day, Buddhi and Balwan. They anointed their foreheads with the traditional Tilak. Buddhi and Balwan appeared to be two emperors rather than two bulls going for a fight.

The two contestants were fed grass and molasses and patted by the political heroes. Guru kissed Buddhi and patted it almost willing it to use its brain while fighting.

Dada patted Balwan from the head all the way down to the tail and conveyed, "You are strong. Use your brawn."

In one voice, all those who were gathered shouted, "Maha Kaali ki Jai" thrice, cutting across all social and political barriers to ask the Mother of the universe for her blessings. Each one gathered there prayed for the victory of Dharma (righteousness) and wanted the guidance of the Universal Mother. The moment had come. Silence prevailed as the two heroes of the day, Buddhi and Balwan charged at each other. The spectators waited with bated breath. The pregnant silence almost spoke in each one's mind that Buddhi and Balwan held the key to the result of the coming election.

Guru and Dada looked at each other trying to read each other's minds as the animals gauged each other's strengths and attacked each other leaving behind a curtain of dust. A keen, close, contest followed and in the end, Buddhi lay lifeless on the ground, most dignified in death. No clapping or shouting followed. Each of the spectators questioned the result of the fight and were sorry that intelligence had lost that day to sheer brawn. Was this a message for them from the Mother to think for themselves rather than follow superstition blindly and remain in darkness and ignorance? That would be the case if Balwan alone ruled the people and Buddhi left them forever.

Their minds swung between the two extremes like a pendulum when they discussed the future of Kinnar that lay in their hands. What should they decide? Whom should they vote for? Guru had a simple charisma without the mass appeal of Dada who could get really emotional and sway people.

When the zero hour came, there was a lot of turmoil in the electorate's minds. Buddhi and Balwan haunted them. It seemed this election was all-important, as the future path and the character of Kinnar and her people depended on the voting pattern. They could choose to be a role model electorate or go to seed like many other constituencies in the past. Very few could sleep the night before the elections. Hordes of thoughts churned their minds but no one dared to talk aloud as this decision was totally the individual's in secret ballot. Many women found their husbands tossing and turning and many husbands found their spouses wide awake.

The Mother seemed to be guiding her children in a strange but certain way by making them think for themselves rather than performing miracles. This, in itself was a novel way of learning. The women were not to be influenced by their spouses or elders in the family. In a democracy, they were individuals in their own right and not doormats. They were equal partners and not subservient to follow the decisions made by the menfolk in the house.

On the Election Day, not a single eligible citizen abstained from voting. Long winding queues ended finally at sunset when the ballot boxes were sealed. Everyone slept well that night without a care in the world as they had done themselves proud.

On the 21st of November, all gathered again in the temple courtyard to hear the election result. Dada looked as if he were invincible. He waved and smiled like a monarch who would acquire the sceptre shortly. He believed that he was undoubtedly the winner and looked at Guru patronizingly.

The TV announced, "A great upset in Kinnar. The seat has been won by the People's Progress Party by a thumping majority."

Guru gave Dada a look which said it all: "People alone are our strength. Omens mean nothing!"

FEELINGS

Kusum looked out of the one and only pigeon-sized mesh window in her 8' x 6' room. It was the only source of ventilation and light. This was the only space she could call her own in this ramshackle house, where she laughed, cried, contemplated and studied. Here, she was herself. She loved her dilapidated bed and the cupboard which had seen better days. The spartan room matched her style of dressing. Today, she was totally oblivious to the beautiful mountains and the lake at their foothills. Usually, they washed away her problems and acted as a balm to her troubled heart through the silent signals they sent her. She sighed and began to compare her life to the setting.

For the tenth time, she remembered Sunil's soliloquy before he had ditched her for-ever like a spineless cur. Death, she believed, would be a welcome relief, especially now, after this agonizing situation. What, or more importantly whom was she living for? No one had rejoiced at her birth and there was no one to mourn her death. This was the price of being born a girl in a lower middle-class family.

Kusum felt she had no self-respect left after the so-called office picnic that Sunil and she were supposed to join. She had been naive to trust him when he had actually engineered the outing for his own selfish ends.

He had smirked and said, "You're nothing more than an old-fashioned, outdated, Victorian prude. You middle-class, glorify marriage and virginity as if they were Gods. The seven pheras (going round the fire) are only the license to enjoying sex and producing bratty kids. In the two months we have been meeting, you should have been burning with desire and passion."

"Frigid woman!" he spat out finally.

This skewed her heart all the waking hours.

An inner voice even now said that she still loved him. After all, he was her first love –a culmination of all her dreams. But she could not have softened and given into him as her values, however middle-class, mattered to her. She had lived by them. As she relived the episode, she could not help laughing at the scene. She had to give it to him that he deserved an Oscar for the way he had delivered the monologue.

She laughed mirthlessly as she thought philosophically that even animals respect some laws, but people like Sunil are a law unto themselves. She wiped the streaming tears with the loose end of her sari.

It was humiliating, no doubt, but ironically, before that horrible moment, she had enjoyed the most magical moments of her otherwise dreary life which she had battled ever since she could remember.

Sunil and she had sat holding hands, on the edge of the most bewitching lake and watched the reflection of the ancient banyan trees. The colourful fish swam swiftly under the water. She had imagined a utopian life that was a far cry from the dreary lacklustre one she had been living. It would have been a great relief!

As she dreamt of her future, she had been suddenly jolted when she felt Sunil pull her sari and tug at the hooks of her blouse. She had instinctively pulled away as hard as she could and fell a few feet away and hit a stone. She hadn't missed the unconcealed passion in his eyes. She ran to a tree close by and had tried to hide behind it. She believed this inner strength to pull away came from the divine powers. Otherwise, how could she, a delicate woman have fought a much heftier person?

Sunil ran to catch up with her and finish his incomplete attempt, but something in her fiery, angry eyes had stopped him and instead,he had lectured her like a pastor and then, when she sat in stony silence, he had slipped away, out of her life like a coward. He had killed something in her forever. As she debated how worthless life was, she realized that her life had been a saga of gender discrimination and suppression. Hoping for a better life with her life partner was a mere myth. When she had been little, she had never had a childhood. She was looked upon as a burden to the family and would cease to be one, once she was packed off to her in-laws' house where she belonged for good or bad. She was being educated as a big favour, but only after she attended to all the household chores, whether there was an exam or not. Her father and her brother Roby sat like lords while Kusum and her mother were expected to dance attendance. Her father would say, "No concessions for you, Kusum, as exams can wait, but we can't. You should be grateful that education for girls is free. Or I would not have wasted money on you."

Her brother added fuel to the fire by adding, "The dal (lentils) is so thick and bland. Your husband will beat you to pulp. Take care."

Sunil, she thought, must be treating his sisters no better than Roby. Ever since Kusum could remember, all the extras in the house came from the money she made by taking tuitions and later on, the salary she brought home. She recollected the number of times she had been discriminated against while her body burnt with fever. When she did not come down to attend on the family, her father would say, "Roby's mother, what has happened to that daughter of yours? Is she feigning sickness to avoid her duties? She is such a shirker."

Roby would rub salt into the barbs by saying that starvation will do her good. Once, he had poured water on her feverish body saying, "Lazy girl! That will teach you not to pretend." This led to her catching pneumonia. Her father said that if she died, there would be one mouth less to feed. "We have my son to take care of us." Very reluctantly, the doctor was called in after her mother pleaded with her father.

Once, her mother had answered her father back and the result was that her father beat her up black and blue and said, "That will teach you to treat me with more respect." Kusum was barely ten when this happened and she had been awake all night, thinking about her mother and concluded that she was no better than a meek cow or pet. She did not know whether to be angry or sorry for the woman who was an ineffective individual in the house, who sometimes showed pity on her. Had she been a wealthy woman, maybe her father would have been nicer to her. The only thing she was not blamed for was not producing a son, because luckily she had.

In her teens, when she was fifteen to be precise, she had attended the wedding of her first cousin. For days after that, in the sanctuary of her room, she romanticized her life with her dream man. He would come all decked up in a shining coat and tight pants (achakan-churidar) with a floral sehra (screen of flowers) to ward of the evil spirits, on a white horse and take her home. He would make her forget all the miserable years she had spent as a second-class citizen. Each of his kisses would wash off each barb she had suffered. She in turn would give all her love, time, earnings and children when the time came. Her home would be a heaven of peace at all times.

"How foolish I had been to dream of a utopian relationship," she thought now.

There was never any respite for her. She thought of the time when she was awarded a scholarship when she got admission in the local engineering college. Her father was in a grouchy mood because Roby had failed his matriculation examination. Roby was envious of his sister and badgered her even more. Her father bemoaned his fate that God had given him a good-for-nothing son. It should have been the other way round so that he would take care of their old-age. Then he could have closed his wayside tea stall and played cards with his cronies all day.

He was no fool and recognized the golden-goose Kusum. She would not need much dowry to be married off and his meagre property could go to his son whose wife would bring a lot of gold, money and so on. These thoughts, he shared with his brother who had come from Mirpur, his village, and Kusum inadvertently heard them.

Before joining college, her mother, under the orders of her husband had lectured her about how she should behave to keep up the family name. After all, her family was doing a great favour by allowing a girl to do engineering. If she had an affair with any male student, she would be reduced to a prostitute.

Her father made matters worse by saying he would get the police to keep a watch on her.

As she cleaned up her room to leave the world a tidy place,she thought of the times when professors had appreciated her efforts and encouraged her. Professor Menon had mentored her because he had recognized her potential. He was a good old bachelor who believed teaching and learning was the only goal in life. He never thought of dating her. She continued to take tuitions right through engineering to stand by her ungrateful family. The thought of her dream man made life easier for her when she was plagued by her family. Roby had taken to drinking and demanded money from her.

In the final semester of engineering, her mentor had spoken to Dr. Gopinath, his close college friend, to give Kusum a part-time job in his manufacturing unit. Kusum was thrilled at this break. She approached her father rather gingerly after giving the month's money from tuitions. After a lot of interrogation, he gave his consent. "But I must talk to your future boss and satisfy myself that you are not up to any mischief."

True to his word, her father met Dr. Gopinath and Professor Menon. He showed his true colours when he said, "Sahib, keep an eye on my daughter. The young can't be trusted. Please see that she does not disgrace me in my old age." Naturally, Kusum was enraged but helpless. She exercised a lot of control to hold back her tears.

Kusum was very happy with her job and Dr. Gopinath was so pleased with her work that he offered her a permanent post. She was to report to Sunil Mittal, the head of the department. Over a period of time, they began to meet for coffee and lunch at a place close by. She began to believe Sunil was her dream man. Her family income increased thanks to her efforts, so her father stopped working.

The bubble burst at that hoax of a picnic. With it, ended her desire to live. When she returned home from the picnic, her father, without looking at her said, "Kusum, go and get ready. Make sure you look attractive. In an hour a prospective bridegroom is coming to meet you."

Roby added his two-bit. He told her that he prayed that the rich old widower would take her away. Half his problems would then be over, and if the old man died soon, then the golden goose could continue to look after all his needs. "How callous can he get!" she thought as she went up to change. "It is from the frying pan and into the fire. After Sunil ruining my life, now I have to go through this punishment of bride-viewing. This is the last straw!"

Her mother came into her room to make matters worse. She brought a new sari, flowers for her braid and glass bangles. "You know, Seth Amarchand who wants to marry you runs a factory. He wants a well-educated virgin. He wants his wife to run the show when he is travelling and mother his five-year-old daughter."Her mother hugged her and said God had answered her prayers and Kusum would fit the bill very well.

The only response from Kusum was to ask who had introduced them to the widower. The answer was that her boss, Dr. Gopichand had suggested him when her father had requested him to help in getting her married. Needless to say, Kusum was dumbfounded.

Kusum looked at Mr. Amarchand and was shocked to see a totally bald, dark, fat man sitting clumsily on the chair her father had rented from somewhere. Kusum's father talked the most. Her brother sat silent for once and Mr. Amarchand asked no questions but stared at her a couple of times. Then he was escorted to the waiting car by the two men. They returned almost jumping with the news that the wedding would take place on the third Friday of the coming month at his house. He had agreed to give some money every month to Kusum's family.

A much-dejected Kusum, dragged her feet up the stairs to her room. A few minutes later, she went out of the house for a walk. She decided then that nothing could tempt her to live. She went to a medical store to buy sleeping pills.

She had just turned to cross the road when a truck knocked her down. Immediately, a crowd gathered. Coincidentally, there was a doctor close by in his car, behind the truck. He took her to his nursing home. Her family came, not out of love for her, but because Sethji was there and he had paid for the three weeks of hospitalization. Kusum was touched and agreed to marry him as she felt obligated. God did not even allow her to die. How much more cruel could He get!

After the wedding, which was a very simple affair, Kusum and her husband went inside their palatial house. Sethji held her slender hand and said,"Thank you Kusum, my darling, for marrying me. It is a favour you have done Anita, my daughter and me. We shall try to keep you happy always. I hope all your thorns will disappear and your life shall be full of roses. You deserve it! By the way, I helped your family with no expectations; so be at peace."Kusum began to cry as no one had spoken such kind words to her, ever.

She thought, "Maybe Amarchandji was the manna from heaven and her family and Sunil were a bad dream."

PRATEEKSHA

Part-1. The growing-up years.

"Silence Please! Time for breaking news! The R E S U L T S. Yes, results!" Immediately, "Shhh... shhh... Silence Please..." could be heard from all directions. Soon, pin drop silence prevailed. Nervous participants waited with bated breaths to know their fate.

The President of the Council for Public Schools, India, Dr. Ashok Singhal, came to the mike to announce the results of the inter-school Debate and Declamation Competition. "Ashish Khan of Mayo College, along with Anurag Barnabas of Rajkumar College, Rajkot wins the second prize with 130 points each! There is no third this year." A big round of applause followed with, "Well done, Mayo! Well done, RKC! Three cheers, Ashish! Great job, Anurag!" Again there was silence and anticipation for the first prize.

Dr. Singhal cleared his throat and announced, "The first prize, a rolling shield and a cash prize of Rs. 5,000 is awarded to Miss Milli Chandran from the host school, Maharani Gayatri Devi School, Jaipur!" The clapping rose to a deafening crescendo as the proud winner marched up smartly to the dais. Milli knew she could not have given a better parting gift to her school, as it was the school's Silver Jubilee celebration. The dowager queen and chief patron of the school, Maharani Gayatri Devi congratulated Milli and said that they were all really proud of her and that her name would be on the roll of honour. Milli personally was very happy with her performance as it was a hat trick.

The same evening, she left school, wearing her school uniform for the last time. Relaxing in the aircraft she thought, "The subject was after my heart and so apt for my generation which holds the torch for the future. No wonder I slogged. I am convinced more than ever about the truth in the subject, 'Irrational, religious and superstitious beliefs slow down human development.'" What surprised her the most was that she, who came from a deeply religious and superstitious family, thought that the pace of development in every walk of life was influenced by irrational beliefs. Her mother visited soothsayers at the drop of a hat. Just as the plane was landing, it dawned on her how much she had missed her family. She could barely wait to meet her parents and elder sister, Anjali (Anju) at the airport.

"I must buy my family gifts from my prize money," she thought, as she picked up her handbag to get off the plane.

At the airport, her family welcomed her with open arms. She ran to them and blurted out the good news and her father lifted her up like he had when she was a child, to see her happy face. Milli laughed and said, "Appa (Dad in South India), I am no longer a kid. I am a big girl about to join college."Her father answered, "For me, you are still the baby I walked to nursery school!"

After the initial excitement of being home waned, life fell into a routine. Anju was busy with her final semester project work and Milli helped her parents out in the family business till the ICSC results came. In the evenings, the two sisters would either stay home listening to music or go for a movie and an ice-cream on Marine Drive. Anju had college friends but Milli had very few, as she was in a residential school. One day,after coming back from work, her mother, tongue-in-cheek, suggested she give some serious thought to planning her career. She suggested meekly, that the family astrologer be consulted too, as they had done in Anju's case.

As expected, Milli was hopping mad. She said, "Amma (Mother in South India), please cut out the Panditji bit."Milli had always been a wizard at maths, so she was bound to do well in anything related to that. That did not need a Pandit. "I'm going for an aptitude test and am going to follow that." Her father, to diffuse the tension said that they better try and check out both.

Milli became high-strung and said, "Appa, for me it is only logic and nothing else. I don't understand why astrologers are consulted for everything and prayers are performed as antidotes. When I met with that accident in the last vacation, why you took to appeasing the stars, I fail to understand! Adversities are a part of life. No more of that ever again for me, please!" She added that she should be convinced logically and not emotionally blackmailed.

Though Milli went ahead with the aptitude test, her mother did consult Panditji and as expected, the former suggested law, and the latter, medicine. So, her parents were not very happy when she opted for law, though she could have walked into any medical college. Milli planned on doing her master's from the London School of Law. She was happy about having won the first round. Indira, Milli's mother, worried a lot about this stubborn streak in her daughter and her so-called logic. She wondered where all this was leading to and whether this streak could be controlled with prayers. Panditji shook his head and said that Milli would not listen and feared that she might get into problems that would lead to a lot of stress for everyone concerned, in the long run. It was not a smooth horoscope, but he suggested that Indira fast on Saturdays so that things would become a bit easier.

So Indira began fasting and Milli noticed, but chose to say nothing, as she was no happier ruining the mood of everyone in the house.

As Anju went about her final semester, her parents began to lookout for eligible bridegrooms. They followed the age-old tradition of getting the horoscopes matched and then proceeding. Anju was very comfortable and did not mind the astrology bit, as life had gone off very well for her so far. She thanked God for her supportive family and the financial security she had, for doing all that she wanted. She always remembered the ten-day trip to Singapore with her friends. Her parents were very happy that she was coming out of her timidity. But Amma said, "Don't travel on a Saturday." Initially it annoyed her, but later she thought, "How does a day here or there matter?" So, she went on a Sunday. In retrospect, it worked out well, as the Saturday flight had engine trouble and came back to Bombay and did not take off again. Since Anju was not adamant, there was more peace and harmony in her life. She was an achiever in her own way, both, in academics and extracurricular activities. Milli adored her but hated her for not opposing superstitions and following religious practices blindly. Milli would at times say, "Anju, you are a coward to not stand up strongly for your views."

Anju would laugh and say, "You are there for the two of us, so why should I lift my little finger?"

They discussed boys, mimicked them and laughed their sides out. Milli would advise her sister to wear a salwar-kameez or jeans when boys came to meet her so that they would know she was not a sari-clad woman and it would avoid sending the wrong signals that she was going to be a subservient wife and daughter-in-law. Anju laughed and said, "Milli, is one's ego to be so big that listening to reasonable requests becomes a crime? No one will walk all over my life; not even you. Don't label people before you give them a chance."

Milli shrugged and said, "You've lost it, baby!"

In November, Arun stole Anju's heart. It was love at first sight. The engagement took place a week after they met and the wedding, a month later. During this blissful period, the two lovebirds spent a lot of time getting to know each other, until a week before the wedding, as it was considered inauspicious to continue their meetings. The two of them had no issues as they called each other several times a day and the florist was more than happy as he was doing good business, with Arun sending flowers daily.

The Chandran household looked really festive and there was excitement all around. Everybody wholeheartedly participated in all the functions. In the few minutes that Indira had to herself, the thought of Anju leaving her naturally saddened her, but she consoled herself that Anju was going only to Calcutta, not USA. She would put the black spot in the instep of Anju's foot to ward off the evil eye. She conducted prayers in the Ashtavinayak temple and Anju's mother-in-law, Malini joined her too. Donations were sent to the family deity in their village near Kanchipuram in Tamil Nadu.

As Anju left for her new home after the wedding, she had mixed feelings, for she was giving up a part of herself for a new journey with Arun. Anju hugged Milli who in turn, to lighten the tense, tear-filled atmosphere said, "Do not trouble my brother-in-law too much or I will be there to cast my vote for him. Anyway, I will come there during my holidays."

Anju smiled and replied, "Milli, from now on you have two homes." Milli could not help crying when the final moment came for the leave-taking.

Later that evening, Arun's and Anju's parents, along with Milli went to the airport to see the newlyweds off to Japan for their honeymoon.

Before setting-up home in Calcutta, where she would join Arun in his business, Anju went to her in-laws' house for a two-day visit. During this visit, Anju's mother-in-law, Malini, asked her to fast for Arun on every Tuesday for life. She had been doing it ever since Arun met with a serious accident in the final year of his engineering. He had had a bad fall from a motorbike and had broken his hand and hip bone. Anju readily agreed as she felt that it was worth doing it for her dear husband's well-being. But she could not help thinking of Milli and what her take on it would have been, and smiled.

One year after the wedding, both the mothers were thinking on similar lines. The million dollar question was - when would they become grandparents? The oracle was consulted and Indira's Panditji and Malini's numerologist did not have very encouraging news. They both said that the couple should wait for a while, as the stars were not beneficial at the moment. Both the parents swallowed their disappointment. A couple of weeks later, Arun rang his mother to say that Anju was coming by the evening flight as she needed bed rest. Their baby was on the way. He told her that Anju would fill in the family with all the juicy gossip when she arrived.

Malini was initially effusive, but in the very next breath she became fearful of the predicted bad period. She felt she should have warned them. Now it was too late. She could not help but daydream about the coming event and forgot everything else.

The doorbell interrupted her reverie and she came down to earth. The happy faces of Anju's parents at the door said it all, and Malini forgot about her oversight.

Chandran asked where the other grandfather was. Then Malini realised how she was totally enveloped in her thoughts and had forgotten to share the good tidings with her husband who was in Delhi. She thought, "If this is the situation when the good news has been announced, then how will it be once the baby arrives... I can barely wait!"

She was able to speak to her husband just as he was leaving for the Delhi airport, on his way home to Mumbai. She told him to wait at the Mumbai airport after he arrived, as Anju was to be received. Of course, Subramanian, her husband, could not wait to reach Mumbai.

So except for Milli, everyone was there to receive Anju and the invisible VIP. Milli came from college and saw the note left for her, "Congratulations, Aunt-to-be!" She was thrilled and on cloud nine and waited for all of them to come home. The happy mood continued as the two families had dinner together in the Chandran household. As dinner was getting over, Anju said that she was advised complete bed rest to avoid any serious complication ,of which there was a strong possibility.

Indira and Malini exchanged anxious glances at the news. Malini said it would be better that she took Anju home,since Indira went to work. She could keep a constant watch on Anju. Indira agreed promptly, as it made a lot of sense. She sent money for pujas (prayers) to be performed in their native place near and got japa (chanting of names of Gods) and homs (fire sacrifices) done for the malevolent stars in the birth charts of Arun and Anju. A month later, Arun came down and when they went for the medical check-up, the doctor said Anju was doing very well and she could go back to Kolkata. Only, she had to be sure to take the medication regularly.

Indira and Malini were not at all happy with Arun's decision to take Anju back to Kolkata but couldn't say much. Chandran told his worried wife to leave the children alone. "You can't run their lives. We are there to support them in case of any emergency." Subramaniam also said something similar when an anxious Malini complained about the recklessness of the young.

Milli was on top of the world as she thought about the baby's arrival and bought all sorts of things that took her fancy when she went shopping. What bothered her was her mother's and Malini Aunty's mania for visiting temples for one thing or the other and getting prayers performed. She said Malini Aunty was lucky to have her sister for a daughter-in–law, and not her. Anju was at least a passive observer. Milli would have brought the house down.

Suddenly, the day after Anju came back to Mumbai in the seventh month, she began to bleed and have severe pains. She was rushed to Jaslok Hospital. Each of the family members was petrified and invoked God's help and mercy. Arun came to Mumbai by the first flight. After a lot of anxious moments, when Anju's blood pressure was falling and the baby too was not in too good a shape, a caesarean was performed and to everyone's relief, a pretty little girl was born. The family naturally rejoiced but couldn't forget the anxiety they had gone through. The party for the little one's arrival was held in the Taj for the near and dear ones of the family, which numbered about five hundred from both families combined. Bright, sunny days with Nupur were a treat and to avoid any more mishaps, prayers were not forgotten.

Milli was upset with all the superstitious beliefs and made no bones about it to her friends. They admired her thinking and knew she had progressive ideas, though at times they were really extreme. She went into her shell at home. She was upset with their elders' attitude and with her sister, for being a party to it all. Her views were heard at the most, but not appreciated. She was her natural, chirpy self only with her darling niece. When Nupur was nine-weeks-old, Anju and she were all set to leave for their home. Indira suggested that Milli go with them to Kolkata to help her sister out. Anju was really happy to have Milli, who she felt was having a rough time coming to terms with life. A break would do her a world of good. Anju felt her parents were at times difficult with Milli and Milli, on the other hand, had no spirit of compromise. No two people were alike and her parents unfairly compared the two of them.

She was glad her in-laws were not really unreasonable, so maybe life had been more than kind to her. Her in-laws were unhappy that she was going back to work, but Anju was polite but firm that Nupur was not going to be left behind with them because she was working. She could manage on both the fronts.

In Kolkata, Milli was elated to have Nupur to herself for most of the day. Mornings, she would baby sit and in the afternoon, go to the National Library and do her research work for her project. In the evenings, the four of them would go out to friends or to eat out. A small celebration was held to introduce the baby to their friends. Milli was a great organizer, which Anju was not aware of and she hoped that soon Milli would settle down, be at peace and come to terms by accepting life.

Milli approved of her sister's circle of friends who were cosmopolitan, young and lively. They were a mix of professional men and women, some single and others married. Among the guests was Pran Goel from Mumbai, a legal consultant to many companies. He was not handsome, but was well-dressed with impeccable manners. As Milli and Pran Goel were exchanging introductions, Nupur's wails were heard from her bedroom. Milli ran up the steps and by the time she brought her niece down, Pran Goel had left. Milli thought, either he must have been bored or who knew, maybe he had a date to keep. "Why bother " she thought and moved on to meet other guests.

A week later, Milli was reading in the library when she spotted Pran Goel browsing through the books. He looked up and saw Milli and came to meet her. They exchanged greetings. He mentioned for no particular reason that he was leaving for Mumbai in a few days. As it turned out, Milli too left for Mumbai earlier than planned, on the same flight as him, as there was no flight available later. The two of them got seats on either side of the aisle so they chatted a bit. Milli's parents were at the airport to meet her and she forgot all about Pran Goel once she started talking about her precious niece.

On her return to Mumbai, Milli became busy with her exams. Her future depended on her performance and she gave it her hundred percent . She was disappointed when she did not get criminal law as her specialization and went in for corporate law instead. She did extremely well in her finals and knew she was headed for London School of Law. That was the easier part. Getting her parents to go along with her plans was the difficult part. They were not always the easiest of people to handle. When her result came, her parents were in Kolkata with her sister. They were thrilled by her result and wanted her to come down but she said no and wanted them to return to Mumbai as she had a lot to discuss with them about her future.

They came and were totally with her about her studying further but they felt she should get married, or at least engaged before she went. Indira was about to say something about the astrologers when Chandran gave her one of those warning looks. So she said instead that it was time Milli settled down like her sister, as she was the right age. That bugged Milli and she let off like the pressure gauge in a cooker. "Stop comparing, Amma. I am not Anju. She is she and I am Milli. Why don't you understand we are sisters, we look alike and the similarity ends there. I don't aim for being a good daughter or daughter-in-law. I want to be guided by my instinct and logic and reach my goals. The stars will not control my life. I am willing to face the consequences of my decisions - good, bad or neutral." Then she said in a moderate tone, "I will marry and have children, for I am not weird, Amma and Appa."

A storm was in the offing as the atmosphere was charged and what havoc it would create God only knew. Her father said in a soft but serious tone,

"Milli, my little one, you have said a lot and we need to digest it. We realise you have grown up and wish to determine your own destiny." He suggested that they sleep over it and talk and review the whole thing in a cooler frame of mind. "The idea is not to hurt ourselves, but resolve problems," he said.

Indira was shell-shocked at the turn of events and went about her daily chores, but her heart was not in it. She was convinced that Milli had a bleak future. That night, the parents talked late into the night and decided that as mature adults and parents they had to behave reasonably and judiciously as they couldn't afford to lose their daughter. Milli was brash because she was young, but they couldn't bring things to a head. A volcanic eruption would do no good to any of them.

Two-three days later, Panditji arrived. He opined that Saturn, the dominating planet in Milli's horoscope was causing all the turmoil. He assured Indira that Milli would marry, have children, achieve fame but that would happen late in life. He said their patience would pay off and that it was the magic mantra. Meanwhile, he asked Indira to regularly put oil in the lamp in the Saturn temple. He also told her to have the Shani Mahamantra (a mantra of Lord Saturn) chanted by a priest forty thousand times. While leaving, he said ,"You can't stop her from going abroad as the time for Kalyanam (marriage) has not come, but for her safety she must do it before she leaves." Of course, Indira did everything as instructed very diligently, but she was uneasy because even Chandran was taking Milli's side. "Oh God, what will happen to my family!" she said aloud.

One morning, Milli came down early and sat with her mother as they sipped coffee and said, "Amma, don't look so miserable and helpless. I don't mean to hurt you or let you down. I will be back with you in two years. It will be good old India for me. I am not exactly an old hag, so my marriage can wait for two years. I don't want to make a wrong choice which may be the case if I settle for something in a hurry. You know I have no one in mind. I may never realise my professional goals if I take the marital plunge now. Then it will amount to cheating myself ." Indira only nodded and said resignedly, "Milli, do what you think is best. I am no one to advice."

Indira and Chandran had to give it to the girl that her arguments made sense and were fair. But she could do with some more restraint in putting her views across. Indira was worried that in England, Milli would meet the wrong person and get carried away and maybe come to grief. Who knows?

The following month, Milli left for England to fulfil her dreams. She was glad she had got a scholarship too, as she did not want to tax her parents more than necessary. Once the decision was made, there was peace and Indira went out of the way to help her in the preparations and had a small party for Milli's friends, as they might not meet for years to come.

Part-2. Milli battles for rational and logical thinking.

Classes began a week after she arrived in London. On the first day, when she walked into the classroom and sat down, there was total silence and she looked up and almost died of shock.

"Oh my God! What is he doing here? Is he a student who is going to sit next to me?"

It was Pran Goel and he was walking up to the dais to take a class. "Its uncanny the way he appears wherever I go," she thought. She found it difficult to concentrate as she thought of the party in Kolkata and the flight to Mumbai. Now, she realised he was in London and would be there as long as she was. It did not take her long to realise what an outstanding teacher he was.

After the class, Pran waited for Milli to come out and they chatted over a cup of coffee. Both of them were surprised at their chance meetings. He did not imagine he would find her there. But he appreciated her choice of the college as it was the ultimate in legal studies by all parameters. He was an alumnus and took guest lectures in international law when he was in England, doing some work for clients. This was almost alternate months.

Milli got busy with her assignments and her part-time job. Over the weekends, she went sightseeing with her friends to Oxford, Cambridge, the Lake Districts and so on. When Pran was in town, they met for dinner. He brought news of his sister and family in Kolkata. Quite unconsciously, she began to look forward to these meetings. But it was on Valentine's Day that she realised he was special when he brought her flowers and a card. She was not averse to this gesture and he in turn thought that Milli was getting under his skin, but enjoyed the feeling. However, he wondered if the future held anything for them.

Milli kept in close touch with her parents, but shared more details of her life with Anju and began mentioning Pran's name often. Anju told Arun about Pran and the way Milli referred to him which made her think there was more to it than met the eye. But he said, "Anju, don't put two and two together, for Milli is a very sensible girl and won't do anything silly and hurt your parents. Come to think of it, Pran has it all, except that he is from a different community. This is the only count on which your parents can raise serious objections and they are sure to, one hundred percent."

It was when Milli was packing to go back to India that she actually realised how much she had missed her parents and sister. But the separation had really been worth it as she had learnt many things and had a Master's degree in which she had topped and also an invitation to join the research team. But what began to bother her was how she would handle meeting Pran in India, with him living in the same city and her parents being there too. In London, it was different. Reality dawned on her that her life was full of confrontations and nothing came without a fight with her parents. She wondered if it was worth fighting for every inch to realise her dreams. "I guess the challenge lies there. This battle is going to be tougher than going to London," she thought. As if it was an indication of the rough going in the months to come, there was thunder, lightning and rain as the cab took her to Heathrow airport.

Her home-coming meant a huge welcome party and the biggest surprise was her darling Nupur clinging on to her grandfather's hands. At three-and-a-half, she was going to a day-care 'Home away from Home', in Kolkata. Anju and Nupur spent the weekend with Milli. Appa and Amma were really happy to have both the daughters home after a long time. After dinner and a family chat, only when the two sisters went up to their room and were talking into the early hours did Pran figure in the conversation. Milli honestly told Anju that she had made no firm commitment to Pran about joining his company. She wanted to gain some experience in another company. It would be good for both of them. Sooner or later, she would raise the subject with their parents.

She was talking more to herself when she said, "Why is life so tough on me! Why are our parents, particularly Amma, so difficult and hung up on consulting soothsayers?"

Anju put her hand on her little sister's shoulder and suggested she see one or two boys to satisfy her parents. That way, she would be making doubly sure Pran was the right person and there was no one else for her.

Milli listened to Anju and saw one or two of the alliances but she felt they did not measure up to Pran. It was not going to work.

Pran proposed to Milli and her reaction was - how would his parents take it? He said he was going ahead irrespective of their nod. "Will you do the same too?" he asked.

Milli replied, "Pran, do you realise that we know next to nothing about each other's families? At least you know my sister and brother-in-law. Anyway, I will take it up with my parents, but believe me it will not be easy. I may have to bulldoze my way."

Pran smiled and gave her a quick hug and said, "Best of Luck, Milli. Remember we are both fighters."

"This weekend the Mahabharat war has to get rolling," thought Milli. "The sooner the better! I might as well get it over with."

"Honesty is the best policy," she thought as she planned how she would go about it. So after dinner when the three of them sat to watch a serial on television, she decided it was then or never. Just then, the phone rang and it was Anju's mother-in-law, Malini, suggesting a very good match for Milli. The boy had all the credentials to be their son-in-law. He was coming from Dubai. He was a distant cousin of theirs and quite a catch. Indira should give it a serious thought. Indira repeated all this to Milli and Chandran.

Milli decided it was the right moment and said, "Appa and Amma, I have something to tell you. Could you meet Pran Goel who has proposed to me? I want to say yes to him."Milli was numb once she had said it. The silence that followed was worse than any words or reactions could have been.

Indira was the first to respond. She said, "Milli, you have ignored our views and sentiments very often. But this takes the cake. Why did you keep us in the dark about your love affair? Have you visualised the problems in adjustment with both the families belonging to different communities? The eating habits, traditions and even the approach to life will be poles apart." After the monologue, Indira looked at her husband helplessly.

He said, "Milli, I am hurt that you chose to inform us rather than discuss everything with us even if we opposed the idea. You should find out more about the family as you don't marry the man, but join a family. Please don't do anything in haste, as it is a question of a lifetime."

A similar but more melodramatic scene took place in the Goel household. Pran made it clear that he did not believe in horoscopes and marrying with rituals. The only person who was pleased was Rajdeep, Pran's younger brother. He was very impressed with Milli, whom he had met once in Pran's office. Their mother was most upset and her blood pressure rose as she said, "Pran, we belong to a community where taking dowry is the practice. What will this girl bring us? Her glad rags? She is a gold-digger and you have fallen into the trap of a sambar-rice-eating South Indian. She will eat licking from her elbow to the palm. There is no meeting ground in our lifestyle. Moreover, I want an obedient daughter-in-law and that she can never be."

Pran coughed to hide his laughter and then said with a smile, "This so-called gold-digger happens to be from a public school, MGD Jaipur, and has studied in London where I studied and am teaching. She will naturally be cosmopolitan, so don't be narrow-minded and judgemental. She is a vegetarian if it helps her cause…"

"Oh, so you are already siding with her," his mother retorted and changed her seat from where she could see her feather-headed son better. She slapped her forehead and bemoaned her fate. At least a Gujarati girl would have been any day better than this Tamilian whose family would only showed off their diamonds, as they lived Spartan lives otherwise. Her final sentence to her son was, "Pran, rather than see this day, I should have died the day you were born. I was so proud of what you have become and boasted about you to our kith and kin. Now Raj will take a leaf from your book and bring a scheduled-caste girl!"

Pran and Milli stuck to their guns but their parents would not budge an inch. Indira was in bed for days and she discovered she had diabetes and her blood pressure was high. Anju came down to see if she could take over and handle the situation. Malini said the Chandrans had given too many liberties to Milli and this was the result of that. But Subramanian said, "You can say all this in hindsight. If Arun had done the same thing what would we have done? Disowned him? In the present situation, Malini, you should be with the family and help them. Milli has not eloped or got pregnant."

While Anju was with her parents, Mr. Goel (Senior) and Pran came over to meet them. Pran did most of the talking as his father, a very reasonable person felt that Pran had to convince Milli's family that she was going to be in safe hands. After all, she was joining their family.

So Pran told them that their's was not calf love. They were adults who knew each other fairly well now for more than two years. They would keep the differences in mind while working on the commonalities. Educated people should show the way. He finished by saying that all that he wanted was Milli's hand and their acceptance. Milli would, with time be accepted into the loving joint-family of his parents and brother. In reply Chandran said, "I hope you are aware of Milli's independent nature. It may be a stumbling block in the adjustments you mentioned."

Pran liked Milli's father's forthrightness, smiled and concluded, "Sir, unless I am proved totally wrong, Milli does whatever she takes on very well and this too, I am sure, she will work towards. Milli is no pushover but with time, she will win over my mother and make her less conservative.

My brother already reveres her and my father has given his blessings, after a lot of thought."

With no choice left, the parents agreed to the wedding which was to be a civil one in the Taj, with a small luncheon for the family only. Anju was the pillar of the family, with Malini helping Indira accept the realities and urging her to take a hold on herself. She liked Pran but thought Mrs. Goel was a snooty woman when she had met her once. Milli wanted to appease her parents in some way for all the misery she had caused them, so she told them that Pran and she would go to the Siddhi Vinayak temple with them soon after the wedding. She went to her parents, hugged them and said, "Believe me, I am totally unhappy about hurting you both so much. I promise you, I will not let both of you down and you will never have to be ashamed of me. I realise how supportive my parents are."

Of course, they were happy that Pran and Milli were going for the blessings of Lord Ganesh. They ardently hoped the marriage would be a success because then, Milli would have vindicated her stand.

Anju made her sister's trousseau and packed it to be sent to the Goel household after the wedding. The wedding was a simple ceremony where after the signing (where Malini and Subramaniam were the witnesses from Milli's side), the sindur ceremony and the tying of the tali or mangalsutra was done. Mrs. Goel did not stay for lunch. Then, Mr. Goel shook hands with Chandran and said that they had nothing to worry about. He reassured Indira with folded hands that Milli was welcome to their family and Pran, his son, would be a good husband.

Then, Mr. Goel left. Pran went with Milli to her parental home. There they all chatted for a while and Pran thanked everyone. Milli reminded Pran that they had a flight to catch, so they had to leave. She left her family, shedding tears. The Chandrans were truly alone now, with both the girls married.

Part-3. Challenges become tougher.

The newlyweds went to France and Britain for their honeymoon. Pran stayed back in London, as he had an urgent case and Milli came back alone as she had to re-join work. Their driver came to receive her. She was disappointed to say the least. She felt Rajdeep could have come because she was coming to her new home for the first time, alone. She could not help thinking that if Pran would have come for the first time to their house, Appa and Amma would have received him. Then she rationalised by thinking that each family was different, so she had to accept the reality. It was easier that way. Her in-laws made polite enquiries about Pran and her. Her mother-in-law did say, "Pran is not here and you are new. If you want something, ask me."

She also added that she was going to her brother's house for a puja and Milli should come. Milli agreed but said she would be a bit late as there would be a lot of backlog in the office. This did not go down too well with her mother-in-law.

Milli kept her word and went to the puja after work, but her mother-in-law was disappointed that she had not come dressed as a bride should be. She thought that all her relations would make fun of her and say that Milli may have come from a poor background, but where was all the Goel finery? Milli did not react and decided time would take care of everything. Priorities of each person and generation differ, so one should give time. She visited her parents after her return and talked to them on the phone daily to reassure them that she was fine. Pran also visited them with her, once he returned.

Pran was keen on opening a branch of his firm and making Milli in-charge. Milli said the timing was wrong for her, as she had just been promoted. He agreed. Both of them travelled a great deal so they had very little time together.

Pran's mother felt that Milli had to be more involved on the domestic front. One day, dramatically she said, "Pran, your wife is not a man!" Pran laughed and said, "Who said she is?" His mother did not see what was funny and continued, "She, as a woman, should give up work, as she is no good in the kitchen. She can't cook. Let her learn that." Pran gently replied, "Ma, give the girl a break. She needs time to adjust. Her presence is required as much if not more, at work. Her brains can't be wasted behind a kitchen stove. If you need help, just go ahead and employ someone, as luckily, money is not a problem."

Not one to give up, his mother continued, "I am surprised at your unstinting support. You don't understand that families where there are no sons and that too a South Indian one, think no end of themselves, with no respect for anyone. If you had brought in a girl from our community, she would have brought a fat dowry, done all the housework and served me well, relieving me of all my aches and pains. Thank God there is Rajdeep to pin my hopes on! I better keep him away from your influence and get him married soon or he may become another Pran."

The festival of Karva Chauth (the fourth day of the moon) was round the corner, two days away to be precise, when Pran's mother cleared her throat at dinner and said to Milli, "You are a North Indian now, so tomorrow you have to fast without a drop of water till you see the moon through a sieve. And then, you must see your husband's face. You can then eat everything to your heart's content after the moon rises. All the women will gather at my brother's house with their puja salver in their festive clothes and jewellery."

Milli was waiting for Pran to say something, but he was a statue by design. So she said, looking at her father-in-law and Pran, "I have never fasted in my life, ever. I will faint at work. There is a very important case coming up for hearing the day after the festival. Can I start next year? I will practise fasting during the course of the year."

Pran wanted to leave the table, but continued to sit. His mother and Milli were both right in their own way. He had not bargained for this. His mother said, looking at Milli, "Pran and you are totally insensitive to others' feelings. If something were to happen to Pran, you will be totally to blame. Do what you like." She walked off in a huff.

After years, Milli shed tears like a child that night. Pran could not believe it and said, "Hey, what do I see? A totally unknown side of you... I didn't know you could cry like this."

Milli was full of self-pity and angry, more with her husband than her mother-in-law and said more to herself that she had fought tooth and nail to marry him and when such allegations were being made he just sat and watched all the fun. Then, facing Pran she said, wiping her tears, "I love you, but that can't be used to blackmail me. I will give my life for you, but not appease God and beg for your life. All my life I have fought superstition."

Pran ruffled her hair and said that he had no issues with her thinking, but he had to convince the old lady. "Impossible," she said and added that she would go for work, but on the way visit any temple his mother wished. "Remember, you told my father that I have to be a part of your family, so I will bend and visit the Mangal-Gauri temple." Pran was proud of Milli. Her mother-in law was in no better a mood than the previous evening. Milli left for work, dressed like a married woman in a sari with the sindur and all. Mr. Goel appreciated Milli but dared not support her in front of his wife. He did smile at her as she left for work.

Mrs. Goel called Indira and told her what a stubborn, useless and badly brought up girl her daughter was. As a mother, Indira should put her daughter in her place by telling her to follow her in-laws' way of life. Malini happened to be visiting Indira. Indira was worried about what Milli could have done that was so unforgivable. Malini asked her not to get worked up and to call not Milli, but Pran. She said that she found him very mature and sensible. Pran asked his mother-in-law to relax, as Milli was okay and not to worry about the teething problems. He also reassured her that his mother would not worry her again.

The Chandrans' hosted a dinner for both the daughters, their in-laws and families, since Anju, Arun and Nupur had come down from Kolkata for Christmas vacation. The three families were cordial enough and Indira gave Malini and Mrs. Goel, silk saris which was their tradition. While leaving, Mrs. Goel asked for Milli's horoscope to check when her stars would change and she would be more obedient and give them a grandson to perpetuate the lineage. Indira asked for Pran's too.

Milli decided to stay back at her parent's place to spend some time with her sister. The sons-in-law went back to their homes after a chat over coffee at a road-side restaurant. The two sisters had a heart-to-heart chat and caught up with all the news in their lives. Their husbands were fine and they agreed that there was no cribbing on that front. Anju said her in-laws were pressing her to have another child, but she and Arun were not too keen. Milli shared her pinpricks too. Anju asked her to have a child and that all the complaints would stop soon. Milli said that Pran and she needed to stabilise the new business they had started and in another year or so they planned to have a child. "A lot of money has gone into the new law firm," she added.

Mrs. Goel asked her sister-in-law for a good astrologer. Her sister-in-law suggested a woman who talked too much and predicted very little. The woman reassured Mrs. Goel that everything would happen in its own good time, as the horoscope was very good and powerful. "That is the problem," emphasised Mrs. Goel. "What can we do to make her more pliable?" The astrologer smiled and moved on to her next project - getting Rajdeep married soon. While she was making her calculations, Mrs. Goel kept repeating, "Please God, don't let what happened with Pran happen to me again. I have lost my peace." What she heard was soothing to her ears -Rajdeep's wife would be from their fold and would be known to her daughter-in-law. The second part was most distasteful and Mrs. Goel said, "We will see. If you are lying, I will see that you are out of business."

The astrologer was very upset with the threat and said in a huff, "If I am wrong, I will give up my profession." On her return from the astrologer, Mrs. Goel seemed to be in an introspective mood and thought about Milli. She thought that in all fairness, she was efficient, caring and extremely self-willed, but not selfish. The next minute, she pitied her son and wondered how he put up with her. She must be driving him mad. He must be regretting his choice. Her mind now went back to the time she was hospitalised for the removal of a cyst. Milli had actually managed the home well, doing three days of cooking and had slept the nights in her room. But when it came to prayers, religious rituals and get-togethers like satsanghs (where people gathered together for religious purposes), she was as stubborn as a mule. Her mother too had come to visit them twice and brought fruits and so on. "The poor lady must have been fed up of her daughter's behaviour. Her sister may be a shade better. I must ask her mother-in-law when we meet next. May be South Indians girls are all like Milli," thought Mrs. Goel.

Milli and Pran went to the US for a two-week trip to attend a conference and take a holiday. Then, in Los Angeles, Milli met her aunt who was a gynaecologist and decided to have a thorough check-up as it was time they planned a baby. Her aunt proclaimed her fit as a fiddle. On her return, she told Anju about planning to have a baby. The pressure was building up on Milli from every front to have a baby soon. Her mother-in-law told Pran, "What else can you expect but no children? You disobey parents in the name of rational thinking, so God is punishing you and us. I will die without seeing my grandchild, only because of you and Milli." Pran was in no hurry and ignored the irrational taunts.

Generally, her father-in-law never interfered, but one day he called Milli away from his wife in case she heard and made Milli's life miserable. He felt sorry for Milli and was convinced Pran could not have got a better girl. They were made for each other. He suggested they try alternate medicine if there was any problem. Milli honestly told him that she was fine according to the US doctors. He was relieved and put his hand on her head and said, "Best of luck, child."

Indira, on Malini's advice, talked to Pran and Milli to perform prayers to the deity who took care of fertility. She asked them to perform a ritual called Narayan Nagbali in Nashik or go to Loni to the Loni Baba who was known for doing wonders after looking through a mirror. One of her friend's son had gone to him and he had told them to throw a green coconut into the sea on a full moon in a particular direction and they had a son soon after.

One night during this time, Pran and Milli had a rather serious, nasty row. It was triggered at a party where one of their close friends, Gita who was a guest too said, "Children are a gift of God. He may be punishing some couples by keeping them childless for sins committed in their previous lives. Otherwise, why would so many people be going to places where they have faith, begging for the pleasure of parenting and holding their baby!"

Once they got home, Pran said, "Milli, I have been thinking over Gita's take on children and your mother's suggestions. It may sound strange and may be shocking too, but I would like to give Loni Baba a try. Nothing may come of it, but what's the harm?"

Milli was totally shocked at the turn of events and retorted in an angry voice, "I am not convinced and to say the least, I am disappointed with you."

Pran did not force Milli. However, he left for Loni the following day without saying a thing. There was such a long queue already. He decided, having come, to wait as long as it would take. He realised that people were afflicted with a million problems and came to seek recourse for them. The Baba must be having something in him if so many people were waiting to meet him even before sunrise!

Finally, it was his turn after a three-hour wait. The Baba asked him to sit on the floor on a mat and asked everyone else to leave. "Thank God," Pran thought.

After a minute or two of invoking the supreme power and staring in the mirror, the Baba said, "You will have one child, but a bit late and it will be a girl. You will face some problems before having the child. You should offer arghya (water) to the Sun and the problems you face will diminish." He portrayed Milli perfectly. Then he said, "I suggest you go to Tamil Nadu with your wife where Naadigranth (an ancient Indian form of astrology based on tantric study), is followed and there you will know if anything else is needed to be done. It will also reinforce my readings. Go and come back with your wife and child."

One thing good about Pran was that he did nothing halfheartedly, so he decided to follow the Baba in totality. His only hitch was Milli. He had to find a way. He promptly contacted a client of his in Madurai, to find out about this Naadigranth and to get back to him about how to go about it.

He recounted to Milli, his visit to Loni Baba in detail, and added that he intended going and would highly appreciate her support as, he couldn't go to the village without her or he would never have asked.

Milli was very distressed and made no bones about it and asked him which woman did not want a child, but that one couldn't go about it irrationally. Medical recourse was the way. "I have no objection to logical decisions, but all this is not fair. I can't believe it is you who is doing all this. I feel trapped," she said desperately. He, on the other hand said very patiently, "Milli, there is a lot of virtue in changing, if the need arises. We don't live in isolation, but with others. Think of their happiness too. A stitch in time may save nine."Milli agreed very reluctantly to join him this once and he was never to bother her again.

His client, Karan Rangaswamy made all the arrangements from Madurai onwards. He drove them to Srinivelli, a village two hours away. There were hardly a dozen huts, very neatly laid out with no touch of urbanization. Each hut had a cowshed with a cow in it and a coconut and a mango tree. No one was curious to know who the visitors were, unlike most other Indian villages where they stopped everything and to come out to see what was happening.

Karan, Pran and Milli entered the first and largest hut, for it belonged to the master of this science. Others who were trained by him lived in the other sheds. Karan came out after prostrating before the man in his sixties, wearing a spotless, white dhoti and angavastra (a piece of cloth that covers a man's upper body).He sat cross-legged with his back straight as a ramrod. He signalled for Pran and Milli to sit opposite him. Milli was uneasy. The man known as Periar (the Master), smiled at Milli and tried to reassure her. He took their thumb impressions and matched them with some manuscripts tied in red silk thread. After some hunting around, he took out a booklet from the bamboo shelves and sat down again. He said, in order to verify that he was on the right track, he would read some information and they had to confirm it because Naadiwas only in search of oneself. He looked at Milli first and said, "Child, you have an elder sister whose daughter is Nupur. Yours is an out-of-community marriage." Then he looked at Pran and said that he had a brother named Rajdeep. "Your uncle was Deepchand, who committed suicide at the age of twenty-four. Your father is Narendra." Both of them confirmed the facts and then the Periar began to read and interpret and tell them that Milli was a very deep and close person who did not share her feelings and views except when she thought necessary. He asked her if she dreamt of snakes often. She answered that it was true. But she was surprised. Pran had killed a pregnant snake and Milli had inadvertently hurt a calf and left it to die in their previous lives.

"There are indications that you will have a daughter, but after appeasing the Serpent God and the cow." Then in an assertive voice he said to Milli, "You are very adamant and it can be detrimental to you and everyone else. Wake up child! "Pran was advised to feed bananas to cows on Sundays, and Milli was to pray to Lord Siva, the Muni Raja, and to Lord Subramaniam on Nag Panchami, the festival dedicated to serpents.

While they took their leave, the Periar asked them to come back anytime they wished to clear any doubts and told Milli in Tamil, "I have only translated; not interpreted. All will be well, as you are a pure soul."

Pran and Milli came out with grave faces and Karan drove them back to the hotel where they had a drink. As the two men drank their whisky, Karan said, "Only the blessed come here and many have been benefitted."

When they were alone Milli said, "Pran, you must be crazy to come here. It is madness, the way all this is done."

Pran said that he was convinced that it was a science and he would like to give it a fair try. Both argued for some time, but neither slept much that night.

A week after her return, to Mumbai, Milli was rushed to Lilavati Hospital with a severe stomach ache. Luckily, Pran was in town. He called his and Milli's mother before admitting her. The senior gynaecologist took Milli into the operation theatre and a cyst that was causing an obstruction was removed. Mrs. Goel rushed and brought some food for Indira who had come from work. Indira's behaviour was correct, but cold and aloof. On the sixth day, Milli was discharged and told to come for a monthly check-up and to ensure that she did not conceive for six months, otherwise, she could have any number of problems.

But for Mrs. Goel, it was the end of the world and every reason to get her younger son married before he went astray like her elder son. Milli had brought only problems! Rajdeep rejected several proposals that came through his mother or her family. Milli decided to come to his rescue and save her mother-in-law more heartache. She had met a sweet-looking girl from her in-laws' community at a seminar she had attended. She asked Pran's close friend, Ankush Goel to check out the girl's family, meet them and give her the feedback. Rajdeep was in the picture and his admiration of Milli went up ten-fold. He was aware of his mother's unforgivable behaviour and hoped things would thaw once he was married. The girl's family formally invited them and when the Goel family were going to meet the girl and visit her house, Mrs. Goel point-blank refused to take Milli because she was an outsider to their community. Rajdeep was stubborn and threatened not to marry or see girls if Milli was not taken. So his mother had to give in, however grudgingly, and they all went, except Pran who was travelling.

A fortnight later, Rajdeep and Usha, who worked for a multinational company, got engaged. Milli hoped there would be some respite for her as her mother-in-law would be busy shopping etc. Usha could not meet Rajdeep before the wedding which was fixed for the fifth of November, as he was travelling a lot for his newly-established business. So the poor girl did not know what would happen to her job in the future.

Pran followed the Periar and Loni Baba with all sincerity. He did not push Milli as she was very touchy and he did empathise with her, but he also felt bad that he could not do all the puja's as Milli was reluctant, to say the least. Now, Mrs. Goel dropped another bombshell.

"Pran darling," she said one Sunday morning when they were alone, "this Milli is no good. Divorce her. She has not given us a lineage. She is an ill-omen."

Pran was livid and said that that was the first and last time she had suggested something so weird. If she did, she wouldn't like the consequences. He walked off in a huff and did not speak to his mother.

Rajdeep's wedding took place with all the pomp and show befitting the Goel family traditions, and more importantly, their status. At the reception, the virtues of an arranged marriage were opined by the elderly women and Mrs. Goel basked in the glory of her perfect second son. Milli was of course ignored. Mr. Goel felt the unfairness of it all and told his wife to stop all the useless gossip and went and sat with Milli and Pran. Rajdeep hated his mother for her beastly behaviour when all the happiness that they were enjoying was thanks to Milli. He got up from the dais after a while and introduced Milli to his friends and associates. The Chandrans were surprised to see a new Milli. She conducted herself with dignity and had never complained to them once about her adjustment issues. Malini and Subramanian were also amazed and proud of her.

The newlyweds did not go for a honeymoon as Usha's grandmother was just a few days away from breathing her last with cancer. The Sunday after the wedding, the Goel family was sitting on the terrace having breakfast. One would think they were a picture of domestic bliss. Mrs. Goel sat between her daughters-in-law. The men stood joking and laughing. Mrs. Goel said amid tears, "God knows how long one lives. I have still not held a grandchild in my arms. Usha, no job and all that for you! First give us a child and be a good wife and most importantly, a dutiful daughter-in-law. Don't follow Milli or there will be only misfortune. Anyway, I think your parents could have been more generous with gifts. If I had a daughter, what wouldn't I have given her?"

Milli walked out of the place as she had had enough of the insane conversation. "Let Usha sit through it," she thought and decided to go to her parents' house and spend the day. She told no one at home. She and her parents spoke to Anju and family. Nupur changed her mood a bit.

Milli watched television in her room. The serial she was watching revolved around having a child and like there was no life beyond. She thought of her very positive attitude to her mother-in-law and how she put up with her caustic remarks. The only reason was that she had married Pran by choice. But it was humanly impossible to not be hurt. She also could not understand Pran's new penchant for appeasing supernatural powers through prayers.

For the first time, she wondered why she was not conceiving. Was it due to biological reasons, or was she really being really punished for being or doing evil? Was it so bad to live by reason? Was she in the minority?

Just then, as she was wallowing in self-pity, the phone rang. It was Pran, most upset at her leaving without informing anyone.

She choked on her tears as she blurted out, "Ask your mother and Usha why I left. Don't pester me. Just leave me alone."

Now Pran was really concerned and said, "Milli, this is not you, my love. You are a better fighter than me. Are you coming home or do you want me to come and pick up my angel? Let us meet at Copper Chimney for lunch."

"No, I am not in the mood," she replied.

Pran promptly put the phone down and came to his in-laws' place and the four of them had lunch at home and went out for a movie. Naturally, the concerned Chandrans were relieved. But Indira worried even more than before, as Milli shared nothing with them. She felt very sorry for her. The doctors now proclaimed that Milli could try for a baby after some medication. She hoped now things would work out for her.

Usha had conceived. Mrs. Goel could not believe her luck. She not only danced attendance on her but wanted Milli to do so too, so that lady luck would smile on her. Rajdeep was now very upset with his mother and her tirades and one day, caught hold of his elder brother alone and accused him of not supporting Milli enough. Their mother was obnoxious and Pran had to stop it. Milli had a heart of gold but could not be taken for granted. "Usha tells me more than you know. Do something before Milli's patience wears out," he told Pran.

Of late, Anju had been suggesting that Milli adopt a child. Later, she could have one of her own too. Anju was very sorry for Milli as the two sisters shared a lot and were very close. She did not want her little sister to face worse music after Usha delivered a child.

Milli thought,"Blood is blood. Would I be able to love an adopted child as my own?"Anju said she would come down and be with her if the situation was intolerable. She could talk to Pran. Milli told her that she could manage, so Anju was not to worry. She would fight her own battles. Anju began to wonder if Milli was building a fortress around her, against the constant taunts.

Pran and Arun were also on the phone often. Pran was all praise for Milli and said that his mother was a real nuisance. "I can fault Milli only for her obsession for logic and rationality. If she bent a wee bit, she would be much happier," said Pran. He said that Anju had been much luckier in some ways, at least with Arun's parents. "Yes," said Arun, as he felt bad for Milli.

Usha's baby shower was conducted with all the attention it required and happy anticipation. So it was a tragic day when Usha delivered a still-born child and was told that she would not conceive ever again. Milli was with Usha all the time, holding her hand, knowing the entire backlash she would have to suffer. Mrs. Goel was busier, bemoaning her lot rather than sympathising with her young daughter-in-law. She, of course did not know about her favourite son not going to have any more children. Milli told Rajdeep to make sure Usha went back to work or she would lose her sanity.

One night Milli let off on Pran, "You are as bad as my mother or yours, getting into superstitious beliefs. Why am I alone being subjected to medical tests and so on like a barren woman? Why not you too? Is the woman to bear the brunt of it all? You all are the same."

Pran was shocked and thought for a while before he answered, "Milli, I have no answers for your accusations." That night Pran thought for many hours and realised that Milli was right about him having a medical check up to rule out infertility from his side. The next morning, before anyone else got up, he left the house to meet the family physician, who in turn referred him to the specialist concerned.

As he was going through the test, a sudden fear and irritation gripped him. He analysed, "Milli is truly fearless and truthful. But can I say the same about myself?" If the report was negative, would he accept it rationally and fearlessly? His worst fears were confirmed. He could barely imagine his mother's reaction and what face she would have before Milli!

Now a doubt sneaked into his mind - of the possibility of his uncle's suicide because he was impotent and hadn't been able to face it. " And what about Rajdeep? Oh my God! How much we men take for granted! Poor Milli! She faced everything for no fault of hers," reflected Pran. In a matter of a few hours, his life had totally changed.

He called Milli and asked her to pack his bag and send it to his office with the driver. She was very upset with her outburst the previous night and wanted to apologise but something in Pran's voice stopped her. Pran caught IA 274 for Bangalore and was received by Anju and Arun, who had moved to Bangalore from Kolkata to expand their business .At their home , he got everything off his chest. It was easier than he thought, but he knew dealing with it was not going to be as easy with Milli in her present state of mind.

Anju told Pran that adoption was an excellent option and that she would take care of everything. She was associated with an adoption agency and arranged for Pran to be interviewed by them and for Milli's profile to be explained to them in detail. It took a while to satisfy their investigative process, but with Anju on his side, Pran was able to make his case successfully to the agency. It was a dream come true when one day, Anju called Pran to Bangalore and placed a cute little baby in pink in his arms.

She also called up Milli who wasn't aware that Pran was in Bangalore and asked her to come to Santa Cruz airport to meet the flight from Bangalore. She told Milli there would be a surprise. "Don't ask any more questions. For once, do as you are asked to without irritating me," she said. Milli was very confused as Anju rarely spoke that way. She was filled with apprehension about Pran's welfare. Why was he in Bangalore? There was no one she could ask.

Pran was relieved that Anju had not left him to handle the baby alone and sincerely hoped Milli would accept the baby with no reservations.

It was a brilliant, sunny morning when Pran walked onto the tarmac alone, with Anju following discretely behind. The baby moved in his arms as he came out of the domestic terminal. Milli couldn't believe what she saw. Pran was walking so slowly and carefully. When she saw the wrapped up bundle she just could not believe it and tears of joy began to stream down her cheeks. Pran came over to Milli and said in an emotionally choked voice, "Milli, Congratulations! You have become a mother and I, a father. She is God's gift to us. I want her to be you all over again, for you opened my eyes."

Milli hugged Pran and took the baby in her arms and said, "You are ours, little one. You made us wait so long." Anju watched the happy family and then as she looked up, she saw her parents, and her in-laws waiting in the distance. Obviously, Arun had alerted them.

They all went over to Anju's in-laws' place. Pran had called his father too, so their whole family was also waiting to see the baby. Mr. Goel said, "Milli, with your and Pran's permission I want to say something. We will call her Pratiksha." Everyone nodded. Mrs. Goel too held her grandchild, hugged Milli and said, "Usha, you must also follow Milli and have a son."

So, the Goels have two adopted grandchildren whom they dote on. Who won in the end - superstition or logic, no one knows!

God's in His heaven and all is right with the world, is all one can conclude.

THE MANGO ORCHARD

Part-1. Bujji's Early Life

Bujji, like many a village lad, had come into the city to eke out a better living. He had been compelled to leave the village because the family had been farming on an inherited two-acre land holding. It gave them their daily bread, but deserted them when there were natural calamities like famines and floods. Once, Bujji's family was almost close to starvation; even a bowl of gruel was hard to get. Naturally, under such circumstances, Bujji could not afford to go to school. But he used the evenings to learn to read and write from the village teacher, popularly called Masterji. Other children were having fun playing marbles or swimming in the pond at that time. Masterji was very fond of Bujji and taught him for free. But Bujji, in turn, reciprocated by taking vegetables from his farm for his beloved mentor. He began to use his reading and writing skills when the village folk received mail and it had to be replied to. His parents' friends, various uncles and aunts in the village, rewarded him with a twenty-five paisa coin and occasionally fifty paisa, if there was good news. This gave Bujji a little pocket money and also endeared him to the villagers of Ambapur.

After two years of drought, Bujji's family sat together and discussed the state of affairs in their family and the village. Bujji's brother Bijli had been struck by polio at the age of five. He could only help cut vegetables or clean rice and wheat but could not add to the family income. Rumi, his twin sister cleaned and worked in the house or lent her father a hand on the land. Her family would not allow her to work outside. They believed the place of the daughters of the house is at home before or after her marriage. So their parents, Kalu and Parvati, decided most reluctantly that Bujji, their beloved child, should go to the city, find work and support the family. Bujji was distraught at the prospect of leaving Ambapur where he was born and had lived for seventeen years. He was saddened to leave the tamarind tree where he spent many happy hours, pelting stones to bring down the raw tamarind. In summer, he ate mangoes with his friends and swam in the village pond. These little things meant a lot to the seventeen-year-old lad and he knew he would miss all these little pleasures. But did he have a choice? He had to leave for Sundernagar as his duty to his family came first. Bujji went to Masterji to tell him his family's decision and seek his guidance. Masterji loved Bujji. The old man put his hand on Bujji's head and patted him. When Bujji touched Masterji's feet, the latter hugged him and Bujji felt he was his true friend, philosopher and guide. He guided him on how to go to Sundernagar where he should meet Ramdhan.

Ramdhan had helped many people from Ambapur. He had left the village twenty years ago and made good in the city by supplying labour to construction sites. Ramdhan had a permanent house in Sundernagar now where he, his wife, a city girl and their two sons lived. Ramdhan took up some small contracts on different sites and made a tidy sum. He would visit Ambapur and pray to the village goddess, Amba for her blessings. He believed his prosperity was due to the divine mother's blessing. For some unknown reason, he never brought his wife or sons to the village. It was possible that he feared that his city-bred wife and his sons would mock the simple villagers among whom he had lived for twenty-two years. One thing Ramdhan did not like was his simple village folk being scoffed at, as deep within his heart, he loved them. No amount of urbanization could make him forget his love for his simple villagers and it would remain so till his last breath. He never forced his sons Manu and Dhanu to visit Ambapur, as they saw nothing good or right about the village. Probably Indu, his wife had brainwashed them. She believed Ramdhan had smartened up after marrying her. He no longer looked a country bumpkin. She used to work as a sales girl in a shop. It was here that she had met Ramdhan, fallen in love and married him. Once he was well off, he had insisted that his beloved Indu stop working. She willingly did so and now lived happily at home. He treated her well. They rarely fought except when he talked of visiting the village.

As Ambapur bid adieu to Bujji, a true son of the soil, it was heartbroken. He was being forced to leave. It had nothing to offer him except abject poverty and misery. All the village folk gave him simple gifts like snacks for the journey, a jar of mango pickle and a hundred rupees that they had all collected for him. Bujji, wiping a tear with the back of his hand, left for the bus stop three kilometres away. He felt he was leaving a part of himself behind. With each step, he moved away from Ambapur. Whenever he looked back to etch his village in his mind, he saw his mother's face. She had told him never to be lured by the temptations of the city. She had also reminded him to send them money regularly. He felt for the address and the letter Masterji had written, to make sure it was there in his pocket. This slip of paper was his passport to the life in the city. It had Uncle Ramdhan's address. He caught the morning eight o'clock bus.

As the bus raced past several villages and fields, his young mind felt less painful about his departure and began to think of his future and dreamt of what it held for him. Maybe he would, with his hard work, become like Uncle Ramdhan, who was a beacon to one and all in Ambapur. He must improve his reading and writing skills, so that he would be respected like Masterji, if he taught in a school a few years from now. Maybe he could come back to the village again someday, who knew? Somewhere along the way, he fell asleep and had to be shaken to wake up at the Sundernagar bus stop. Poor Bujji was disoriented as he got down from the bus. He had a steel trunk in one hand and in the other, a bag that had a basket of food. He got down and looked around him and found a tea stall. He walked up confidently and ordered a glass of tea. The owner, almost his age, chewing pan, asked, "Plain or masala?" Bujji didn't know the difference, but said, "Plain." The owner realized that this customer was not worth paying attention to, so he slapped the glass on the table and said, "One rupee fifty paise." Bujji thought, "In the village it is only fifty paise," and walked away. He asked someone how far Bapudham was. The man said, "It is very far, one hour from here. Take bus number 21 from the station, which is a five minute walk from here." Bujji followed his instructions and got into the bus after a half an hour wait. It was close to one when he reached Ramdhan's house. Bujji felt proud of Uncle Ramdhan when he saw his house. It looked nothing like the houses in the village– even the headman's, which was the pride of Ambapur.

Bujji knocked on the door and waited. Ramdhan came out and said in an authoritative voice, "Who is there?" Bujji gave Masterji's letter to Ramdhan. Ramdhan called his son Dhanu and asked him to read. Dhanu said, "Baba, Masterji has asked you to help Kalu's son Bujji." Ramdhan's mind went back to the village and recollected how Kalu had helped his father, Dhanulal when he had needed rice and oil during a drought year. Then he thought of himself, two decades back - how he had come alone to this city and had no help at all. It had been rough going for him, while facing so many hurdles. It was then that he swore that he would help anyone who came from his village by finding a job for him. Here was one more boy at his doorstep.

He said, "Bujji, I remember you very well. I hope everything is all right in the village."He gave Bujji some water to drink and asked him to wait outside. He told him that he would take him to Mandir Lal and see if he could be employed on the construction site.

So Bujji waited under a gulmohur tree opposite Ramdhan's house. He was not asked inside. He did not understand this, as in the village, everyone was free to walk into each other's huts with no reservations at all. A guest was treated like a God.

"How long will I wait?" he thought. "Where will I sleep tonight?"

Just then he heard a feminine voice break into his thoughts. Indu, Ramdhan's wife said, "Have you brought any money to last you a few days or do you expect to live off my husband? All of you are the same, with no self-respect. You all live off us like parasites, as though we owe you all this hospitality."

"Chachi, I have a hundred rupees with me," Bujji said, "I don't know how long it will last me. But I promise to give you every month some money if you tell me how much you want."

"You seem to be different from the others from the village," said Indu, "Don't tell your Chacha but give me five hundred rupees over a period of six months. He doesn't understand how difficult it is to live here and wants to do service free for his folk. I have to educate my children, Manu and Dhanu in good colleges and we might have to give money to the principal to get admission. Remember Bujji, in the city, people are not human. Money and power are the gods they worship. Here, people do whatever they want to by hook or by crook. They are selfish and ambitious. Your Chacha wants to be a god, so we are like this, begging."

Bujji thought of what his Chachi said, but he could not understand the begging part of it when he saw the big house. He thought that all said and done, it was better here in spite of the politics of the city dwellers. How could they be beggars when they had such huge palaces? He said aloud, "Chachi, I promise to give you Rs. 80 every month for five months and Rs.100 in the sixth. I will run errands for you on a holiday if you help me now to settle down in the city."Bujji did not know that contractors gave a commission to Ramdhan for finding them good workers. It was his livelihood. He would go round to neighbouring villages and at times to the city's slum colonies and locate the people and get them employment, of course for a price. So both parties gave him money.

Indu was elated and said, "Bujji, you are like a son to me,that is why I told you about the money. I will go inside now. Your Chacha will come out shortly." Bujji wasn't able to figure out Indu's thinking, as he was thrown into an unknown world. In a few hours, his life had changed totally. Being young, he was not depressed but a little apprehensive of what would happen to him. Ramdhan came out and took Bujji with him, on his two-wheeler, to a construction site quite far away. A block of flats was under construction. Bujji waited outside while Ramdhan went into a shed. It was a site office, where the supervisor, Mandir Lal sat on a steel chair opposite a table that had plans, blueprints and a model of the to-be-completed apartment block. Bujji saw the two men laughing and talking over tea, which was brought in glasses by a ten-year-old boy. He was beginning to panic now about getting the job. How would he get along in this lonely world far away from his dear ones? On second thoughts, if Ramdhan was doing well here, he too could succeed. Things had been worse for Ramdhan when he had come to this city. As he pondered over his new life, he knew he could not go back for quite a while, as his family needed his financial support. As his mind was mulling over the radical changes in his life, the two men came out and walked up to him.

Bujji got up and walked up to them and folded his hands, while Mandir Lal looked him up and down and said, "Okay, leave him here, Ramdhan. If you recommend him, I will take him on. I will try him out for a week and if he is useful and good at his work, I will retain him. I will pay him twenty rupees a day."

Ramdhan put his hand on Bujji's shoulder and said, "You are lucky, my boy. People don't get a job for weeks. Don't let me down! Work hard. Come home sometimes."

Bujji shook his head and saw Ramdhan leave. Now he felt really alone in this wide new world and imagined that he was being thrown to the wolves. Mandir Lal told Bujji to pick up six asbestos sheets and make a shed for himself. He also told him that Manoj and Sukhia would help him. A tall, well-built man came from the back of the building which was under construction and Mandir told him, "This is Bujji, a newcomer. Help him build his shed. Make him water the building and carry material."

Thus started Bujji's life in Sundernagar. Being a quick learner, he was popular with the twenty odd people on the site and was really happy. As promised, he gave Indu Chachi eighty rupees and sent three hundred rupees home. On alternate Sundays, he went to Ramdhan's house and shopped for groceries and vegetables for them. He rode a cycle given by the contractor for his use.

Once Bujji paid off the five hundred rupees to Indu Chachi, he started saving the money in a post office. Ten months later, the building was completed. They moved to the construction-site of an independent house. Bujji was now a permanent employee on a monthly salary of eight hundred and fifty rupees a month. He thanked his sahib, Mandir Lal, whom he had come to admire greatly. He asked for ten days' leave before he started working at the new site, to meet his people in the village. Mandir Lal agreed. Bujji's mood was buoyant as he went shopping in the bazaar for his family. He bought a sari for his mother, a kurta for his father, clips and bangles for Rumi, his twin and for Bijli, he chose building blocks because Bijli had a very sharp brain which he could put to good use, though he could not move about very much. It would help him pass his time playing and innovating with the building blocks. With the passage of time, he could learn to draw plans on paper, which Bujji could show his employers. It was a good investment, he felt. He remembered his mentor, Masterji and bought him a pen.

He could barely wait to get off the bus as he approached Ambapur. On arrival, he recounted his life in the city to his family and friends. The family heard him with pride and awe and they knew he had done them proud. He noticed the house looked better, as did the family. The kind of lunch they had laid out for him had never been eaten before, which showed that they were comfortably off. There was dal, vegetables and phulkas with homemade butter. Bujji was satisfied with what he saw and his family made him feel like a king. His wish was their command. For the first time, he realized what money could do. His father saved money every month for Rumi's wedding. Bujji wanted to send Bijli to a good hospital for his leg next year. Masterji was overjoyed to meet him and gave him a cup of tea and biscuits. He talked to Bujji as an equal and asked him everything about the city, his life and finally about Ramdhan. He also told him how Kalu came and gave him fresh vegetables from the farm as before. While leaving, Masterji said, "Bujji, don't be satisfied with your achievements but keep on improving to become a successful man. One day, I hope you come back and take over my mantle. It is my dream."

On the second day after his arrival, Bujji sat in front of the hut in the cool evening breeze and saw sheep coming home. Young boys followed them with crooks in their hands. They drove the mute animals into the grassland and brought them back in at sunset. He was wondering what life had in store for these teenagers. Would it offer a sedentary life or something exciting and novel that could transform the village with the construction of canals or tractors for tilling the land?

While he was busy in his thoughts, his father came and intruded saying, "Son, we are really proud of you. Thank you for standing by us. People look up to me with a new respect today. I'm called by the Mukhia (village headman) for advice. It is all because of you. Yesterday, Bhagat Kaka came to meet me and brought a marriage proposal for you. Nalini is the only child of Sattu, the shopkeeper at the end of Temple Street. I want you to see her and give your opinion before you leave."

"Baba, what is the rush? Let me work one more year and then consider marriage," Bujji replied. Kalu said, "Son, you need someone to keep home for you, so that you get more time to work and earn more. I suggest you see the girl before saying no. Don't refuse without seeing the girl. Good and beautiful girls from decent families are not easy to find."

Bujji went back to the city, engaged to Nalini, a rare beauty. He would get married four months later during Diwali. Bujji dreamt of Nalini day and night. She became an obsession with him. He wished she were literate so that he could write letters to her and get to know her better. He was determined to teach her to read and write. He worked harder to make a little extra money that would be welcome once he was married.

Bujji planned to make constructive and effective changes during his lifetime to eliminate gender inequality in his village. "Women can be empowered if we educate them. The home will be built on a stronger foundation and they can be bread winners if the need arises. That is my dream for Nalini. My father and his peers never studied or barely did, and mother was there to cook and keep the house. Sadly, few men think in this way, so women are not decision makers. I wish to do something for my sister. Maybe now that I enjoy a different respect, I should speak to father and send Rumi to Masterji, to start reading and writing. If we men can't help women out from suppression and bondage, who will?"

The new site, 'The Mango Orchard', was a mango grove off the main road. It was full of moderately high, but fruit-bearing mango trees. The mangoes were accessible to passers-by. The king of fruits was in abundance when the construction began. This was the first house to be constructed. Unfortunately, a few trees were being felled to give way to sell as plots. The owner was a Sethji, who came in a posh car with his wife who looked like an actress. Bujji had seen such people only in the few movies he had watched. He got intense pleasure in watching the Sethji tick off the supervisors.

The four months flew and his supervisor, Mandir Lal, gave him fifteen days leave to get married. Mandir Lal promised to give him a raise of a hundred rupees, since his responsibilities would undoubtedly increase. In turn, Bujji would have to write some accounts for him. He laughed and said, "Bujji, now that you have someone to cook and keep home, you could spare some more time for extra work."

"Sahib, you are always very kind to me. Are you married? Where is Bhabhi?" Bujji asked Mandir Lal, "Don't you ever go home to visit your wife?"

Mandir Lal looked out of the office room and his eyes became misty, as he said, "Bujji, my Pushpa died in childbirth two years ago. I left the child with my parents. I just can't look after him. My Pushpa was an excellent wife and we were both madly in love with each other. I went crazy after her death and could not see the child who is her replica. I came back to work here.I felt it was better to keep him away from me. I can't love him though it is his birthright. I feel, however irrational it may be, that he snatched away my Pushpa from me. I don't know fair or unfair but he should have gone and Pushpa should have been spared. We could have had another child, but no way can I get another Pushpa. I hope your wife brings you all the luck and happiness which my Pushpa gave me. Here is a small gift for you." He took out an envelope and gave it to Bujji.

Bujji could not believe life could be so good to him. He thought Nalini, his Nalu was the Lakshmi (Goddess of wealth and prosperity) of his life and that's why she was coming to make their home on Diwali. "Just as lights illuminate the space around them, may my Nalu bring with her all the sparkle and luck we can ever want into our lives," he thought. Like for most people, Bujji's wedding brought him joy and happiness. He suddenly felt very responsible as a householder. He thought how beautiful Nalini looked as a bride. "She looks a hundred times more beautiful today than four months back," he thought. He took his bride to the village temple and asked for the blessings of the Goddess. He caught Nalini's hand and held her close to him. A week later, the newlyweds left the village with two boxes. His father-in-law held his daughter and son-in-law close to him and said, "Bujji my son, take care of my darling daughter; she is more precious than my very life. Her mother and I have never said a harsh word to her. Be kind to her."

In the bus, it was different for Bujji than the first time when he had gone to Sundernagar, because this time he was not going alone. He had a job and a bright future ahead of him. Nalini was quiet as she had left the only world she knew and was on the threshold of entering a new world about which she knew next to nothing. Though she was nervous, she felt she could trust Bujji and he loved her. Bujji said nothing but held her hand as if he read her thoughts and wanted to reassure her. He admired her doe-shaped eyes and wondered if anyone could be luckier than him. He could not believe lady luck was shining brilliantly on him. He swore to never let Nalu down. They reached Sundernagar and got down and went to the same tea stall where he had ordered a plain cup of tea, hesitantly, the first time. This time he walked confidently with his wife and said proudly, "Two cups of masala tea."

The stall owner smiled and said, "Just married?" and handed over a few biscuits and two cups of steaming hot tea. Bujji spotted a photographer close by, had a photograph taken and got into an autorickshaw with their luggage. In a matter of forty-five minutes, they reached their destination. He saw Nalini's eyes light up as she saw the hybrid mango trees on both sides of the road. The trees were more like bushes and the leaves were a lush green with a refreshing smell.

She said, "The air is so fresh here, like in the village. I will be happy here."

Bujji said, "I'm glad you like it, but we will not be here forever, you must remember. We will move from one site to another."

Nalini had her head covered as she got down. Mandir Lal came out and broke a coconut in front of their shed and welcomed them. He joined the couple for lunch. Nalini opened the lunch box her mother had packed and the three enjoyed the sweets, rotis, curry and pickle. Thus began their first day in the Mango Orchard. Nalini was very happy cooking, cleaning and spending a lot of time in Bujji's company. They were in ecstasy whenever they were together. The newly-weds enjoyed total bliss as the stars lit up the sky. The starlit nights brought with them new messages and signals for Nalini and Bujji who were perpetually in the seventh heaven in the Mango Orchard. They sat under the trees gazing at the magic moon, singing folk songs or sharing a joke or their beautiful dreams. Nalini did not want to have children for another two years. She wanted to learn to read and write so that her children would be educated and become good citizens. She wanted to bring her parents and in-laws' families to the city and live happily. Bujji could not believe his good luck. But occasionally, he felt uneasy about such a beautiful wife. He wished he had a beautiful house like Ramdhan's far away from his workplace. He did not like the way his fellow workers talked about other girls and women. Mandir Lal frequented their house more than he would have liked. He could find nothing wrong in Mandir's behaviour, yet he was not comfortable. Nalini was innocent and saw nothing amiss. She loved the orchard and spent many hours there when people worked on the site. Bujji felt he could work when Nalini was safely under the trees.

One day, Mandir Lal called Bujji and said, "I can trust you totally. Can you go to Sethji's house and get some money urgently as the labour have to be paid? I'm not well today or I would have gone myself."

"Okay," said Bujji, but did not like to leave Nalini alone. Sethji's house was a little far away. It was an hour and a half's ride by cycle. Bujji went,completed the work assigned to him and returned at an unbelievable speed. He was relieved to see that all was well. He thought his fears were unfounded and that he was overreacting and so he settled down to a carefree, normal life.

Nalini and Bujji went out on Sundays to the market and made their simple purchases. Nalini enjoyed these trips because Bujji and she joked, laughed and argued like kids when shopping for things. Bujji always had an eye on the purse, whereas Nalini would get carried away on seeing trinkets, so they had their pleasurable quarrels. Bujji always gave in to her whims, as she was the only child of her parents and had never been denied anything by her father. Sometimes, they paid their respects to Ramdhan Chacha and Indu Chachi. Nalini would help Indu Chachi with household chores, so she was more than pleased with the couple.

Nalini began to learn reading and writing Gujarati from Bujji. They enjoyed these times together as he would tell her stories or make her count leaves, birds, fruits and bags of cement to be able to do simple sums.

It was a Sunday and Nalini was cooking lunch. Mandir Lal called Bujji to his office. The former was on the phone. "It must be Sethji," thought Bujji. Mandir Lal told Bujji that Sethji was coming to take him to the nursery to pick saplings and bring them here to plant in the bungalow. Mandir Lal would go for ten minutes to order cement bags for the compound wall. Sethji came and picked up Bujji and gave money to Mandir Lal for the cement. Sethji was a kind man who treated his employees well and respected them. His wife would, at times, pack something to eat for Nalini.

He was generous with tips and took good care of his domestic servants at home and the labour in the factory. In passing, once Sethji had mentioned to Bujji that after this house was complete, he would see that he would be shifted to his factory. That is exactly what Bujji had hoped for.

Nalini was invariably sad when Bujji left her alone to run errands for Sethji or Mandir Lal. But at the same time, she was proud of her beloved husband. She thought he was very clever and could not only read and write, but could teach her as well. But the most outstanding quality in him, according to her, was his broad-mindedness. He educated her and did not want her to cover her head. He never raised his voice and was very understanding. She appreciated the confidence Mandir Lal had in Bujji, so she did not mind making tea for him or a snack once in a way. But she heard Bujji grumble, "Why can't he let us alone? Doesn't he know two is company and three a crowd! He is a real hang around."

Today she decided to practice her writing and reading to please her husband, a very strict teacher. She locked her room and happily walked into the orchard and sat in a cool spot in the interior of the orchard. She began to read the story from the book Bujji had bought her. She read the interesting story of Prithviraj Chauhan and Samyukta. She carefully underlined some of the words she did not understand, so that Bujji could explain them later. While reading, she began to dream of her future. She wanted to not only teach her own children, but also the children in a school in the city. "I am too slow," she thought and resolved to work harder.

As Nalini dreamt of her future, Mandir Lal returned to his office and began to think of his lovely wife Pushpa, who, he irrationally convinced himself, was killed by his son. He thought how lucky Bujji was to have Nalini who was charming, gentle and beautiful. She was enchanting. "My Pushpa would have liked Nalini. How can I forget my Pushpa! Some tell me to marry again, but I can't. Who knows, the other girl may also die. He remembered a fortune teller say, "You are not lucky in love." I may be tempting fate by remarrying. Or Lady Luck may be wanting me to take the plunge again. If Nalini had a cousin sister in the village, I would ask her to introduce me to her. How complicated life is!"

He was lost in his thoughts when suddenly he heard a faint cry of a woman from the distance, "Help! Help!" This was repeated with, "Ma . . . . . . help!" He shouted, "Where are you, who are you? Wait, I'm coming!" He ran in the direction of the trees to the right. It took him a little time to reach the interior. He saw a man running towards the road. He could only see his back. He was dumbstruck when he saw a trail of blood. The man was running away holding his bleeding hand.

There was silence. He looked around for a second or two and then it struck him like lightning. "Oh my God! Where is Nalini? I should have checked her house. The voice asking for help sounded familiar. No, no, it is someone else. I must help, whoever it is," he thought and ran to see. His feet were rooted to the ground at what he saw. His hair stood up. Nalini was on the ground, her blouse torn, her sari dishevelled and a gash on her forehead. He could not believe what he saw. Suddenly his mind ordered, "Run, run! Nab the culprit!" The man must be a maniac. He felt his feet were heavy as iron as he chased the man. But to no avail!

He ran next to the site office and shouted for Tariq, Mohit, and Chunnu, "Come and help me." By the time they came, he ran to his house, opened his trunk and dug out a red sari, his Pushpa's memory of her wedding day, and ran to the spot. The three boys who were alerted followed Mandir Lal who ran like one possessed. He was ahead by a few steps and quickly covered Nalini with the red sari. He could not believe how serene and beautiful Nalini looked in death. He could only sympathise with Bujji, as he had gone through the pain of losing his beloved. "Poor Bujji! How can I help him avenge Nalini's death? That culprit deserves a dog's death if there was one. He should be tied to a post in the marketplace and whipped to death. I won't leave him!"

He sat outside his office as he waited for Bujji's return. He needed to be alone to get a grip on himself. He drank water, washed his face and sat in the shade. "Will Bujji blame me for sending him with Sethji?" Tears rolled down his face when he recollected the day he got the news of Pushpa's death. "Oh God! Why are you so envious of the happiness of the poor that you snatch their beloved? Are you cruel to the rich too? At least, they can console themselves that they have money and power. We, the poor, don't deserve this!"

His mind was in turmoil. Suddenly, Sethji's white car turned the corner and stopped in front of the house. Mandir Lal's stomach had butterflies as Sethji called him to get two boys to unload the plants from the car. He dared not look at Bujji as if he had done something wrong and went to Sethji and spoke in bits and pieces rather incoherently. Immediately, the latter stiffened and called Bujji and held him close and told him what he had heard from Mandir Lal and walked with them to where Nalini was lying. Bujji was wailing all the way. On seeing Nalini, he became inconsolable.

A minute later, he looked at Mandir Lal. The look on his face was one of a lunatic and his eyes were balls of fire as he said, "You stabbed me in the back. You did not protect Nalu. Why? Or are you the culprit? In what way had I provoked you that you took it out on the innocent one?" Mandir Lal was stunned and showed the trail of blood which was almost dry now and said, "Bujji, my brother , if I were the killer, I wouldn't be here. I would have run away like a coward. Think! Why would I put Pushpa's sari on her? Why would I behave like an animal when you are like a brother to me? You can ask the boys where I was all morning. When I heard a voice cry out for help from a distance, I was in my office."

"Mandir, Bujji," said Sethji, "we can't change the tragic event. Please take my Matador and go to your village with the body. The last rites should be in your village. Bujji, whenever you return the job is yours."

Part-2. Bujji picks up the threads of life again

By four o'clock, the Matador reached Ambapur with Mandir Lal, Bujji and Chunnu. Bujji was in a daze. He only said, "Nalini, what happened? If only I had been with you... What will I tell my family and my in-laws who entrusted you to me?"

The villagers were wondering what happened when they saw a vehicle coming. What honour was being conferred on them? Had a movie star come? Masterji came out of his house and saw the vehicle. The doors opened and Mandir Lal and Bujji came out. The villagers saw Nalini's lifeless form and a pall of gloom set in. Bujji heard and saw nothing as he sat in front of his house in a corner. All the villagers had gathered there. Mandir Lal briefly explained to the two families what had happened. Mandir Lal returned in the vehicle once the cremation was over. Some of the villagers wondered why Ramdhan was not with Bujji.

Bujji was numb. He walked up and down the courtyard like a zombie. At times, he would say to himself, "Nalini, I took you from here as a bride and I have brought you back lifeless. Why did you do this to me? I thought you loved me! Couldn't you live just a while more to tell me what happened? Where will I find your tormentor and murderer so that I can..." At times he would laugh, an empty laugh and cry at other times. Nalini was gone ten days. That day, Ramdhan came to the village and said he was not well. He had met with an accident, so he could not come earlier. He had a bandage on his hand. He was shedding tears for what had happened. He blamed himself for neglecting the daughter of his village. "Kalu, I have let you and our families down by not keeping an eye on the children."

Bujji spoke to no one and sat by the village temple in Ambapur. One day, he saw two women coming into the temple. He overheard them say, "Nalini died so young, just over a year since she got married. What kind of a man is Bujji? Can't he protect his wife? If she was wayward, he should have kept her under control. A man must be a man. What happens to these men who go to the city, we don't know! Ramdhan Bhai's wife doesn't come here even once and Bujji's wife is killed." Bujji's eyes suddenly opened. He was shaken up by the talk of the womenfolk and decided to leave that moment for the city and begin working.

It was easier said than done. The family was totally broken. He was the pillar of the family so they could say little to console him. They wept for him and felt he did not deserve what had happened. They wanted him to stay awhile. With time, the wounds would heal. He was bound to come round and marry again.

But for now, he was like a living ghost. He had built a wall of silence around himself. His twin, Rumi, grieved for him as though she was him because they were twins. The night before Nalini's tragic death, she had been restless and had dreamt of bad omens and cried. Kalu wanted to go with his son, but Bujji only said, "No, Baba." There was a pregnant silence and Bujji became unapproachable.

Nalini's parents, Sattu and his wife were going about like demented souls. They had nothing to live for. They blamed their fate. The cruel goddess had punished them. But for what they didn't know. They cried unabashedly when anyone visited them. "Nalini, you are here. You can't go." Slowly they limped back at a snail's pace to the daily routine as the business of living has to go on. Time and tide wait neither for the mighty nor the nonentities.

The shop was opened again, but with no dreams of Nalini coming home to them and their pleasure of having a grandchild. Sattu used to look out often in the past and see if Nalini was coming to meet them. Now, that had become a dream forever. Kalu's family got back to the land and to looking after the cows and the hens they owned now. They did not have a word of rebuke for Bujji. Bujji left one morning without telling a soul. He went back to Mandir Lal who ran to hug him when he saw him walking up the gravel-road. Bujji worked, but not as before. It was mechanical, as if his soul was lost. Mandir Lal took him under his wing, as he would his own brother. Mandir Lal wrote regularly on the first Sunday of each month to Bujji's family – like a son. Masterji would read the letters to Kalu.

A month later, one night, Bujji asked Mandir Lal, "Tell me, how did the shadow of the man look?" Mandir Lal said that he was not sure, but the culprit appeared to be tall and had on a dhoti and turban. Bujji nodded. Gradually, he began to change and had a strange expression but most of the time he had a faraway look. At times, he talked normally about Nalini. Sometimes, in his sleep he kept talking or shouting, "Nalu, I can't live without you. Tell me who and I will kill him. Please say something or take me to wherever you are."

At such times, Mandir Lal would soothe him. One day, both went for a walk and there Bujji ran after a man shouting, "You are the culprit. Nalu told me in my sleep." He got at the man's neck when Mandir Lal pulled him away and told him not to lose control of himself. He must take a grip on himself and not hallucinate. Nalini was at peace in heaven and she should not be disturbed. The two returned home. Mandir Lal was shaken up at what had occurred during the walk. He decided not to say a word about it to a soul, as Bujji might be put in an asylum. Bujji was okay for two to three months, so Mandir Lal breathed a sigh of relief that all was well.

But his relief was short lived, as Bujji would laugh or cry hysterically. Mandir Lal, after a lot of serious consideration, confided in Sethji. Sethji asked him to take Bujji to a psychiatrist after he had fixed up an appointment. After two or three sittings, the doctor suggested admitting Bujji in an asylum, as he could be dangerous to society. Sethji was willing to pay for the complete hospitalisation and medical expenses. He informed Bujji's family and asked them to visit their son sometimes. He assured them that they would continue to get money each month as usual.

Thus began a tedious and long journey of recovery for Bujji who could not make out why he was in the mental asylum. Why was he far away from the mango orchard and from Nalini? Mandir Lal spent each Sunday with Bujji, as he was now working in the factory. Bujji was not put in a dormitory like the others but in a room. He ate, read and worked on the new hospital building project. He was on medication including tranquilizers when he became very listless. This went on for a year. Sethji visited him once in two months to reassure him. Bujji did not want to see his father because once he suggested remarrying to cure his mental state. Bujji went through numerous sessions of unburdening his mind. The doctor worked on him. He quite liked Bujji and explained to him that the idea of revenge was worth pursuing if it had a purpose. If he could identify the culprit then he could bring him to book. In Nalini's case, it was futile. The doctor promised to write about the incident in the papers with Nalini's photograph. Bujji had her photograph which they had taken when they got off the bus on reaching the city. He gave it to the doctor. Gradually, the loving care of the doctor put him on the road to recovery. Bujji talked to the inmates cordially, which got him friends but he was afraid of the world outside. It was scary. The words of the women near the temple in Ambapur drummed in his ears and haunted him like a ghost. He vowed never to return to the village.

One day, Bujji was asked to meet the superintendent of the asylum. He told Bujji he could go back to his normal work as he was perfectly okay now. As a precaution, however, he should come for annual checkups. Bujji asked for a medical certificate and went to Sethji and requested him to take him on permanently, as that is what he would like. That way, he could educate himself and teach in the premises of the factory and fulfill many people's dreams. Sethji complied. Bujji believed Sethji was a living God.

A few weeks later, Bujji saw in the local paper, "Ramdhan Sawant held for rapes and murders of three innocent women." The sentence given was hanging. Bujji couldn't believe what he read. Ramdhan asked the jail superintendent to permit him to see Bujji as his last wish. Bujji looked at Ramdhan's face. Bujji could not believe he was the man who had reduced him to a demented person. He said, "Chacha" and Ramdhan came closer and held his hand and broke down, as he confessed everything. He had a weakness for women and had eyed Nalini whenever they came to his place. He could not see her as a daughter. He debated whether he should try to keep away from the temptation or give in to his carnal desires. The latter of course won. "I watched your moves and struck at the first opportunity. I killed her because I did not want any proof of my animal action. But she was strong and hit me on the arm very hard with a stone. My brute strength got the better of her. I totally underestimated a woman's inner strength to defend her honour. In her, I met my match."

Bujji could not believe what he heard and was sickened. All that he said was, "Chacha, God is punishing you, but that's not enough. You should be hacked in public." Just then, Mandir Lal came and was not happy to see Bujji there. He said, "I wanted to be with you Bujji, so I came here. I had a gut feeling I would find you here after reading the paper. I'm glad you are okay."

Ramdhan pleaded for forgiveness and said, "Our families have stood by each other. So please help my sons. Soon they will be fatherless." Then Bujji said, "Chacha, for what you did to Nalini you deserve no help. God knows what is good for each one!"

The following day, Ramdhan was hanged. Somehow, Bujji felt better and at peace with himself.

With time, the scars healed, but not enough for Bujji to marry a second time. Mandir Lal married Bujji's sister, Rumi, who brought back his son born to Pushpa and took good care of him.

Three years later, Bujji's father fell in the fields and became bedridden. Bujji's filial duties brought him back to the village. Masterji had retired, so Bujji took his place. Most unexpectedly, Bujji felt an inner peace, as he went about his daily chores. "Strange are the ways of destiny," he thought on Nalini's seventh death anniversary. "I had never imagined myself back in the village when I married and much less, after Nalu's death." Nalu's parents refused to stay with their son-in-law. But they gave Bujji their money to start a library in Nalini's memory.

A woman has the power to influence her better half and the reverse is true as well. A man can go to seed because of a woman or stand by her memories and live a praiseworthy life like Bujji did. While we hear of women braving all that happens after their husband's death, a man can also exhibit qualities of great fortitude.

RAAKHEE

Rajee Khanna delivered a baby boy at 11.30 am on 24th August, 1951. "What is so great or unusual about that?" one may well ask. True, but for Rajee, a typical middle-class Indian housewife, it was the fulfilment of a long, cherished dream. As she held the two-hour-old baby in her arms, the agonizing labour pains became history. It is an understatement to say that Mahesh's parents were overjoyed too. The grandson was much awaited since they already had a six–year-old granddaughter, Munni. Rajee and her in-laws were more than happy that Kunal, the baby would carry on the family torch. The chapter of taunts for not having a son had come to a close. Though she doted on Munni, Rajee's son would be a crutch when her hair turned grey, face wrinkled and she became toothless. As a mother, Rajee would love Munni no less than her son, but Munni, after all, was a girl and would get married and leave to set up her own home. Rajee was glad that now her peers and elders would respect her and most importantly, her son would send her to heaven by lighting her funeral pyre.

Lying in a comfortable private room of one of the best nursing homes, she wondered how ecstatic Mahesh, her husband would be to see Kunal, their son. She wondered how the Queen Bee, her daughter, would take to her little brother. Would she be reluctant to share the attention with her sibling or would she accept him easily? One could never be sure of human reactions. Rajee fell asleep as she pleasantly thought about the future. The baby too, wrapped up in a blue sheet, was asleep in the crib near his mother. The two made a picture of peace and harmony which any photographer would have loved to click.

Mahesh and Munni peeped into the room and tiptoed inside. Munni went straight to the crib and peered at the new born, while she clutched her father's hand. Having stared at the little one, she looked at her parents. Rajee who was awake, smiled at Munni and beckoned her. Munni kissed her mother and said, "Mummy, Daddy, the baby looks like a monkey. Look, he is looking at me." She squealed with joy as Kunal opened his eyes. "Can I tie him the raakhee? (a multi-coloured thread tied on the brother's hand by the sister, on a special day known as Raksha Bandhan) Daddy, I must explain to my new friend, Michelle, what a raakhee is and why the multi-coloured thread is tied."

Mahesh was nonplussed by Rajee's complaint that he had forgotten her in all the excitement of Kunal's birth. He laughed and said, "Impatient as always, my pretty face." Quietly, he brought out a fabulous bunch of white and yellow carnations from under the chair and gave it to her saying, "Thank you,my fair lady for giving me a son. The family is complete now with a beautiful daughter and a handsome son." These words enthralled Rajee as they were music to her ears. All day she had been dreaming of this.

Little Munni repeated her question about tying the raakhee a little impatiently. Rajee lovingly explained to her daughter that the baby was too tiny for her to tie a raakhee. His skin was still very soft and tender. She suggested that Munni tie it to one of the corners of the crib. "Darling, next year you can make him sit on a chair and tie the raakhee. I am sure he will love all its colours and the attention he will get."

Munni tied her first raakhee, a colourful red and green silk thread to the corner of the crib and looked pleased with her achievement. Mahesh kissed his daughter and gave her a lion-shaped pencil box from Kunal in return for the raakhee. That night, Munni cuddled up to Mahesh in bed and put her head on his chest while Mahesh narrated the significance of tying a raakhee. Just as she was about to fall asleep, she said, "I will tie a raakhee every year, but will Kunal give me a gift every year?" Mahesh ruffled her curls and said, "Yes, my little one, always. It's a promise."

In this way, the expression of love and the bonding between Munni and Kunal began. Mahesh made sure he chose lovely gifts for his beloved daughter and gave them to Kunal to give his sister, whom he idolized. On the day of raakhee each year, Munni took out the silver tray and put a raakhee, sweets, kum kum and a silver lamp with a wick. She lit the lamp and made Kunal sit on a small stool. Unlike his usual restless self, he sat still as though he knew that something special was taking place. Munni put a long tilak on Kunal's forehead, tied the raakhee on his right wrist and put a sweet in his mouth. He enjoyed the special attention paid to him and gave his sister the traditional gift with a flourish.

Years rolled by and on each Raakhee festival, the above pattern repeated itself till the year Kunal left for a hostel in a private residential school in Rajkot, located in Gujarat. He was now eight. A week before raakhee was to be celebrated, Kunal looked at his diary, where he had marked in red, the 20th of August as the day of the Raakhee festival.

He called his father and reminded him of raakhee and the gift for Munni. Mahesh said, "Kunal, I am truly proud of you and Munni. She has already mailed you a raakhee and the gift from you is ready." Munni did not open her gift till Kunal came for the holidays. The parents were touched by these small but sensitive actions of the siblings.

Munni's marriage was fixed, when Kunal was about to start training as a marine engineer at the Directorate of Marine Engineering Training at Kolkata. It was a coincidence that the date of Munni's wedding, Kunal's birthday and Raksha Bandhan were on the same day. The Gods seemed to have blessed the family thrice. Usually, Indian festivals do not fall on the same day of the western calendar, so this was an unusual occurrence. This year, the house wore a festive look with all kinds of flowers and orchids specially flown in from Mumbai. The entrance of the house and the patio floors were painted with rice paste and other coloured powders in artistic designs. Rajee personally planned and supervised these traditions to the last detail. True to her nature, she perfected everything, be it a kitty party or a wedding. Munni got up well before dawn and got ready to tie the raakhee. She hoped her lazy brother would not need a splashing of cold water to wake him up. She prepared a mug of tea for him and was on the first step of the staircase when she looked up. What she saw made her almost drop the tea. Kunal was coming out of his room. He looked stunning in his sky blue kurta-pyjama. He beamed at his sister as if to say, "I beat you to it."

But when he saw Munni, he became emotional due to the telepathy they had, though they were not twins. He quickly controlled his feelings and came down the steps and said, "I thought I would be told to make my own tea." Seeing the mug in Munni's hand, he pulled it and sipped the steaming hot tea. She laughed and gave him a loving whack.

As Munni tied the sacred yellow and red thread, she couldn't control her tears. She thought it would never be the same today onwards. Kunal's eyes misted too and he hugged his sister and said, "Silly, don't cry. You have two homes from today, not one at the cost of giving up another. You are lucky that your future home is also here in Surat. Next Raksha Bandhan will be at your new home." Just then, their elegantly dressed parents joined them. As always, Mahesh handed over Munni's gift to Kunal. Kunal smiled and said, "Dad, from next year I will buy the gift for Munni. I will get my stipend from the next month and the scholarship money as well. I hope it is okay with you." Mahesh smiled his approval and Rajee was really proud of her son who was more mature than any of her nephews and nieces or even her friends' children. His winning personality made him popular with people of all age groups. He was keenly aware of the challenges his father had had to face to make the business in Surat a success and the respect he enjoyed in professional and social circles as an upright man. Kunal upheld and applauded these values too.

Rajee looked at her daughter with mixed feelings that day. Every mother dreads the thought of her daughter leaving her home. Munni leaving them seemed unimaginable to Rajee. "What would her new home be like? Obviously a happy one! Why doubt it?" she thought. "Rohan seemed to be what any girl would hope for. Yet, who can look into the crystal ball? Well, well," she thought, "Munni is no uneducated, docile woman but one who is capable of handling the future with tact and astuteness. Unless of course, I am totally wrong. What will I do without her?" She thought and wiped away a tear. "The future is to be lived, not fantasized," she concluded. She moved on to look after the guests who were coming down for breakfast.

Mahesh was miserable at the thought of Munni's bidai (departure). Home was unthinkable without Munni's laughter and chatter. He hadn't slept a wink and wished he could turn the clock back by twenty-four years.

After the wedding celebrations, uncontrolled tears flowed before Munni's bidai. The trio, Mahesh, Rajee and Kunal, were left to cope with the silence in the house. Each of them put on a brave front, but was missing Munni more than words could express. Mahesh put on Munni's favourite music. This made him feel even worse, so he switched it off and all three of them began to play Scrabble. Mahesh said that he wished Munni were here to tease them and boast of her excellent vocabulary. Rajee suggested at the end of the game that they talk to Munni to check if she was okay. But Mahesh and Kunal vetoed the idea. Just then, the phone rang and all three rushed to the phone but Rajee made it first and spoke to her darling Munni between tears. This way, they all began a new chapter in their home, with Munni moving over to her new home with Rohan. After all, the mind plays a huge part in the acceptance of situations, but it is tough when it is related to one's children. These changes are neither rare nor unnatural. In fact, eyebrows are raised if children do not get married and start their own lives and move on. These mixed feelings are only to be expected whether a daughter-in-law joins the home or the daughter leaves her parental home.

A year later, a few days short of Raakhee, Kunal called his sister to say he was coming over to her place for the day. "I have already sent you my raakhee," said Munni and between repeated apologies and embarrassment, told her kid brother that she was leaving with Rohan for a holiday to celebrate their first anniversary. She added that she would be leaving another raakhee with their mother. Kunal talked to her with all the chirpiness he could muster and said, "It's okay, silly, don't fret so much. I am sorry I could not plan earlier. But I will surely miss you."

After this conversation, Kunal swallowed his disappointment and rationalized the whole thing. He went shopping for his sister for the first time in his life. At Park Street, he bought a musical compact for his sister's raakhee gift and a crystal bowl for the couple's anniversary. He got back to his room, put some clothes in his travelling bag and boarded the train to Mumbai and later caught a connecting train to Surat. Mahesh and Rajee waited anxiously on the platform for the train to pull in. It seemed like ages, though the train was on time. Kunal being eager to meet his parents, was standing at the door, waving frantically to catch their eye. Mahesh and Rajee were overjoyed to see Kunal after eight months.

They had organized a surprise party for Kunal's 18th birthday. All his friends from school who had not left Surat were there. The three of them missed Munni and Rohan a lot, and Rajee was vocal about her disappointment. She felt Munni could have planned better. Mahesh chided her gently saying that Munni had to share her time now, so Rajee should not be too harsh on her. He said that he was very sure Munni was missing them too and thinking about Kunal.

As if on cue, the phone rang and Kunal and Munni chatted away as if they were on their favourite couch and not on the phone. The telephone department sure made good money off the half an hour call.

*　　*　　*　　*　　*　　*　　*　　*

A few years later, Kunal had come home from the ship for his 25th birthday. By then, Munni and her family of three had moved from Surat to Kotgarh in Himachal Pradesh. They now had a little daughter, Lalita, who was three. Rohan was into business. He had set up an apple juice canning unit. Munni enjoyed being among the hills in the apple orchards with the fresh air bringing in a total feeling of well-being. She treasured the peace she found in the mysterious mountain terrain whose magic touched one and all. After a year now, she was glad to be away from the mad urban hustle and bustle. Initially, she had not been too happy to leave Surat, as she was emotionally attached to it. She couldn't think of a life beyond Surat and her family. But that was in the past. Now, she didn't like to leave the hills for too long. She and Rohan decided to surprise Kunal and her parents by joining them for Kunal's birthday celebrations. The joy they had spread with their presence was written all over the faces of Munni's parental family when they rang the bell. Little Lalita stole the show. Her grandparents indulged her every wish. Just as in the past, Munni tied the auspicious raakhee thread on Kunal's hand, which was now a grown man's hand. When they both looked at each other, it seemed like time had stood still and they were still kids. They hugged each other and Kunal quietly slipped a diamond ring onto his sister's delicate finger and she exclaimed, "Wow! That is some gift, little brother."

Rohan was really glad that he had been able to give his precious wife this joy,though it was at the cost of skipping an important meeting. He thought that money could always be earned, but such occasions and the happiness that they brought with them came once in a lifetime. The truth is that time and tide wait for no man, so one should never wait for another time. After all, money can't buy or replace what comes from the heart. Rohan was a worthy son-in-law, equally committed to the family values that Rajee and Mahesh had inculcated in their children.

In this emotionally-charged environment, Rohan walked into the rose garden and his thoughts went to his childhood. He thought of this rare bonding between a brother and sister through a thread, ornate or otherwise. It offers security and protection to the sister. He remembered his Raksha Bandhans with his sister, Beena. Once, he had nursed his sister back to health as a teenager after an attack of jaundice. Their parents had gone on a holiday to celebrate their silver wedding anniversary. Beena had hugged her brother tenderly and said between tears, "You are the best brother in the world." Even today, she wrote long, expressive letters, especially for Raksha Bandhan.

"I wish she would come more often to India from the West Indies," he thought wistfully. She made rare visits to India after their parents had died in a car accident soon after her wedding. She wanted to escape the memories of the tragic event. But her brother felt lonely at times like this. Munni was keen to go to Beena's place next winter when Lalita had her holidays. Beena kept in regular touch with Rohan, Munni and her darling niece whom she sent regular gifts for raakhee from her son Somesh, as well as birthday gifts.

The following year, Kunal married Neha. The newlyweds visited Munni. Lalita was in a residential school in Simla, so the house was quiet. She came over for the weekend to meet her darling Kunal Uncle and her new aunt. When the time to say goodbye came, Munni hugged her brother and suddenly, Kunal heard a sniff and stiffened. He looked at Munni and said in a serious tone, "Hey, what's up? Why have you become sentimental? I promise to be there whenever you need me."

He wondered what had brought on those tears; problems with money, health or Rohan? Munni wavered for a minute and then decided to go ahead and said, "Kunal, Rohan is braving a strike and threats to our life from the union leaders single-handedly." Immediately, Kunal cancelled the tickets and informed his company to extend his leave by a week.

Rohan and Kunal burned the midnight oil for three days, reading old contracts and reconstructing new ones to suit the present crisis. The union leaders were highly impressed by the support Rohan enjoyed from his family and came to an amicable settlement. The womenfolk were busy in the house making jams and juices. The extended trip gave Neha a chance to know Munni better. Neha was floored by the love and support she found in her newly-acquired family. Such strong ties among siblings were new to her, as she was an only child. Rohan and Neha hugged each other and he said,"You have a brother in me now. We are one family." Munni's eyes twinkled and she smiled this time as she bid goodbye. Neha promised to send a raakhee to Rohan every year.

It was the morning of 16th August, 1986, when Munni got up to the incessant ringing of the phone. She was awakened from a terrible dream. She said "Hello" in a drowsy voice. The tone of her father's voice from the other end shook her out of her sleep and the news that followed, sent a shiver down her back. Her father sounded anxious and slightly incoherent. He asked her to rush to Mumbai as Kunal was being flown in from New Zealand in a serious condition and her help was required. He had met with a serious accident in the engine room of the ship and had suffered severe burns on his hands and leg. Neha was with her parents as she was to deliver her first child in the next month. She too was on her way to Mumbai.

Munni quickly got herself organized and talked to Lalita in her boarding school. She left a message for Rohan who was returning from Brazil that day, hopped into the car and got the driver to take her to Delhi to catch a flight to Mumbai.

All the way on the flight, she could only pray for Kunal's recovery. She believed he would be smiling and make light of the situation and tell them that they had overreacted. She vowed to take Kunal to holy places the next Raakhee. When the plane landed in Mumbai, she was the first one out on to the aerobridge and ran all the way to a cab. While in the cab to Breach Candy Hospital, she thought of her parents. She stopped the driver to pick up a raakhee and flowers, as it was Raakhee and Kunal's birthday too. After the day of her wedding, this was the first time that Kunal's birthday and Raakhee had fallen on the same day. (Kunal's birthday was celebrated as per the Gregorian calendar based on the solar year and Raakhee, is celebrated as per the Hindu calendar which is based on the lunar calendar. So, Hindu festivals do not fall on the same Christian calendar dates year after year.)

In the hospital, Munni tiptoed into Kunal's room, just as she had as a little girl, when she had come to see her mother and a new-born Kunal years ago. Rajee was near the head of the bed moving the basil beads in her hand. Neha was shedding silent tears. Munni could not believe what she saw. Kunal was on a raised bed and was breathing with the help of an oxygen mask. His face was calm. She went close to him, touched him and tied the raakhee to the bedpost, as his hands were covered with bandages. She applied the red tilak on his forehead. He seemed to acknowledge it with a slight movement of the head and a smile playing on his lips. Almost immediately, he breathed his last and on the same day that he was born, he left the world. It was a strange coincidence. He seemed to have been waiting for Munni and her raakhee.

The only consolation for his grief-stricken parents was Karan, Kunal's son, who was Kunal all over again. Neha remarried, but made sure her in-laws saw enough of Karan. They were still fit enough to manage on their own, so they visited Neha as often as they could. They accepted her husband, Govind wholeheartedly.

Munni has not got over the loss of her brother yet, but has learnt to cope with it. Kunal's memories help her to carry on with the business of living. Beena visits her brother, Rohan often now, as she realizes what Munni is missing. Rohan visits Neha very often and Lalita and Karan are pretty close.

It is sad that all Rajee's hopes in Kunal were nipped in the bud. But she is really happy that Rohan is more of a son to her and less of a son-in-law. Ultimately, Rajee and Mahesh will move to their daughter's home in the hills.

Man proposes, but God disposes. Mahesh thought he had given Rajee the most wonderful son but how their daughter turned out was one of life's wonders.

MEENA'S HOME

Meena was going through a book of quotations and proverbs for a talk she had to give to an all-women's group -'Rainbow' on 'Parenting - A Joyful Experience'. As she flicked through the pages, the well-known proverb,'The hand that rocks the cradle rules the world', caught her attention and she thought, "Does it really? Yes, but to a point only. Rocking the cradle is easy but parenting is another story. I don't know if parenting is any more difficult today, with the change in perceptions of age-old values, and joint families giving way to nuclear families. Outside influences tend to substantially score over family influences today, than they did in the days gone by. Much higher exposure and awareness through the media is a major cause for this."

She looked out of the window and recollected her daughters, Bindu and Mohini playing throw-ball almost thirty years back and what she used to think then. Bindu was older to Mohini by about two years.

"What will Bindu and Mohini grow up to be like?" she would wonder from time to time. She cleaned the dust on the glass of their framed photograph and realised how the years had flown, leaving only memories behind. Her daughters were so charming and loving Time sure flew. It seemed like yesterday that they were toddlers wearing identical clothes. "I wonder what life holds for them. How far will they study? Will they have professional careers or will they settle down being homemakers like me? I don't know, so it is best I wait for the future to unfold itself. Then I will sing or hum the popular song -'Que Sera Sera...'"

Meena came back to the immediate present and thought about the subject on hand. Her mind went back to her childhood. She thought, "If I were to talk of my childhood to 'Rainbow', I would say…

I was fortunately born into a family where girls and boys were given equal opportunities to study and participate in sports and social events. Gender discrimination was unheard of in giving opportunities. I, like my brothers, went to an expensive residential school. I was expected to do well in academics and concentrate on leadership that went hand in hand with outdoor activity. Also, discipline was given a very high priority. On the other end of the pendulum, my parents held conventional and slightly orthodox views. We touched the feet of elders to seek their blessing and visits to temples were a frequent occurrence. Birthdays meant a mixed celebration. First, we visited a temple as thanksgiving and then had a party at home with a cake and all the fanfare. It was a happy mix of the Eastern and Western cultures where I could study in a co-ed college and go out with boys. Yet, love marriages were unheard of for both boys and girls. It had to be an arranged marriage for all of us."

"That's pretty impressive, Madame Meena," she told herself and laughed.

Coming to Bindu and Mohini, it went without saying that the influence of Raja's family was really conspicuous which meant that her maternal family's impact on them was almost negligible.

"That was the home I knew before I married Raja. My in-laws' family was a generation ahead of the existing society always. They had no qualms about defying unreasonable social practices and talked of their revolutionary stand with an element of pride. Aunt Leela was educated at a time when society expected a woman to be within the confines of the house. Child widows like cousin Neeru and Aunt Pami were made financially independent and were encouraged to join the mainstream of society. This is saying a lot. Neeru did her graduation and taught in the local high school and Aunt Pami did a music course and taught children classical music in the school and at home.

Aunt Suhasini told us often about how she had lost her husband at the age of twelve. Her world had come crashing down. She was Raja's favourite paternal aunt and everyone doted on her. Their father fought the womenfolk and close friends and ensured that she was sent to school, and then to college subsequently in Madras (Chennai). She went to Sri Lanka to attend a seminar with her college. Maybe she was the first to do all this in their society and state. She became a lecturer in the local college. The only thing that our family did not dare to do in that era was see her remarried. Not so much for the fear of being ostracised by society, but, because boys from decent families would not come forward to marry a widow even if she was a virgin. All these bold decisions were really commendable.

Even in our generation, very few widows remarried as society did not take too kindly to it. For that matter, unhappy marriages did not end up in divorces either. Marriages were a happy mix of arranged and fewer love marriages. Love affairs were taboo and were accepted grudgingly after a child was born. Women and men drank beer with no reservations in a small town like Thandavuru, to which my in-laws belonged. This was the early sixties. Needless to say, there were not too many families who were like my family.

I married Raja in the mid-sixties of the twentieth century. He and I belong to the same community and caste. Both, Raja's parents and mine spread the word around of their intention to see their children married. Some friends suggested suitable families. A common friend, Gopal Uncle, made a suggestion to both our families. The horoscopes were matched by my parents, as they genuinely believed in it and not as a ritual or formality. With Raja's family, it was the opposite. They asked for my horoscope not because they had any faith in it, but because Raja's father wanted to use it as an excuse to say that they couldn't accept the proposal,in case his son did not like me. He did not want to hurt his friend, Gopal, who had suggested the match by saying, "My son did not like the girl." He would have rather blamed the stars since they couldn't protest. He need not have worried. As Raja claims, he fell head over heels for me the minute he saw me. The astrologers declared that our horoscopes matched perfectly, much to the delight of my parents. My father went from Madras to Thandavuru and formally invited Raja's family to visit us and meet me and the rest of the family.

While my father was away, the rest of us enjoyed imagining the meeting between Raja's father, Mohan and my father, Venu in the following way and enacted it too.

Venu, my poor Dad, would enter the gate of Mohan's house wondering if he should shake hands or fold his hands when he met Mohan. Shaking hands may be too western. After all, as the girl's father he would be thinking, 'I can't take liberties shaking hands as it can be misconstrued.'

"Come on Venu, we are all westernised enough to shake hands, I am sure," his inner voice would say. "Venu, I can't imagine you, a lion in the office and a leader among your social circle being so helpless."

"I know, my dear," he would say to his inner voice, "but remember, this involves my precious daughter? If anything goes wrong, my real lord and master, Sulochana will never forgive me. My darling wife will nag me till my last breath. I will play it safe or I won't hear the end of it for a lifetime!"

"So, you agree easily that you are the president of hen-pecked husbands?" the inner voice would tease him.

"Have I ever denied it?" he would answer.

"Oh Venu, then the answer is simple. Make a call from a public booth to the home department," the inner voice would advise.

"No," Venu would say."I will play it safe and fold my hands. My inner voice better keep quiet as I have a mind of my own; even though it may be a weak one at times."

Finally, when he would ring the bell, Mohan would end Venu's dilemma by extending his hand. Much relieved, Venu would begin his well-rehearsed speech a bit nervously. It would look as if he were attending an interview for his first job. Gone would be the self-confidence of so many years. He would say,"Mr. Mohan," and then clear his throat and feign a cough and begin.

"Some water for you, Mr. Venu?" Mohan would ask like a good host. Venu would politely refuse saying,"You know the custom of the girl's side - not taking even water till things are decided. I am not in favour of all this, but women are different. I have been well-instructed by the home department."

"Come on Mr. Venu, we are all modern. Do not stand on formality. Take it easy. If I had a daughter I would have been more nervous than you are." Dear Venu would continue with the task on hand.

"I offer, sorry… propose, my daughter Meena for your elder son, Raja. Please do come to our house to meet our family and see the girl. It will be an honour for us to play host."

"Mr. Venu, please relax," Mohan would laugh.

All of us were in fits of laughter, as I stood enacting the roles of both the people involved.

In reality, it was a very informal meeting where the dates for the meeting were fixed and my father helped with the train schedules and so on.

A few weeks later, Raja and his family came over to Madras. I had heard that Raja was not happy about going to see the girl formally. He thought he was no one to pass judgement on an unknown person. He abhorred the idea of the poor girl being paraded. However, his parents wanted to follow the customs for want of a better alternative.

I remember now, how the house was spruced up for the visit. My mother was visibly nervous and very edgy. I could not understand why, as entertaining came easily to her and she enjoyed it immensely. Later on, I learnt that my mother was worried about how would she tell the boy's parents a 'no', if I were to reject him. This was a privilege only the boy's family enjoyed.

I was cool about the whole thing. I was certain my parents would not force me to say yes against my will. Well, everything ended well and both families were full of smiles. Raja and I spoke on the phone often during the four weeks before the wedding. After the wedding, we, like any other couple, had to make changes in our lifestyles and thinking, as we were the products of our respective upbringings, exposures and experiences.

Raja believed our daughters ought to be treated as individuals, and be brought up to be fearless and face all the challenges of life with confidence and courage. He wanted them to become outstanding career women in a male-dominated society. He believed in discipline but did not push it too much. He felt that values were to be integrated in their upbringing through interaction rather than strict adherence to rules. Often, our daughters, the apples of his eyes were indulged in. He was particular that whenever they spoke any language, it had to be flawless. Their gait had to be straight. He made Bindu walk with a book on her head. She extended it to walking on the road with a book on her head, much to the amusement of onlookers. Anything they took up ought to be done thoroughly and to the best of their abilities. That was the bottom line.

I agreed with Raja to a point but felt that ultimately the girls had to run a home well too, along with the demands of their professions. They couldn't be encouraged to not step into the kitchen and ignore the house. My friends and I felt Raja that overdid the professional bit and he had to make them realise their roles at home too. Raja ignored my views and pampered the girls silly and they, of course, loved their father for being on their side. I felt strongly about all this upbringing, especially when I had to struggle alone when the domestic help was not there.

Raja hardly ever talked of marriage to the girls. On the rare occasions that he did, it was to reassure them that this home was always theirs and if the need ever arose, for any reason after marriage, they were welcome to come back. He would tell them to never give up their economic independence, or they would feel trapped and wouldn't be able to make the right decisions. He would quote examples of people like his niece, Lata who did not walk out of her unhappy marriage because she could not support herself if she opted for a divorce. She did not have the ability to earn money, so she put up with all kinds of mental and physical indignities. Raja overdid this and Bindu was scared of not performing well in academics and hence, not getting her dream job and disappointing Dad. She was under a lot of pressure before her college exams. Mohini was a happy-go-lucky person and argued with her father that a career was not everything and wasn't the key to one's happiness.

I had got married at nineteen and naturally had to make many adjustments in my thinking while parenting our girls. Over the years, Raja and I agreed on many issues, but there were some on which we didn't. I continued to believe strongly about the need for the girls to share domestic chores in the house and involve themselves totally in the celebration of festivals. I felt that it was the only way to retain our culture and traditions and also pass them down to posterity. Raja rarely helped in the house and did not encourage Bindu and Mohini to help me either. I certainly felt cut up on this count, as I had to do everything myself, single-handed, even when my in-laws came to stay with us. I felt as if I was one up against the three. I always prayed and hoped that the girls would marry in our fold even if it were a love marriage. I believed families must not give unlimited freedom to children, as they could go wayward. But Raja invariably supported the girls if I complained to him or talked to them.

When Bindu completed graduation, I would bring up the subject of boys, relationships and occasionally marriage. Bindu often laughed off what I said or argued illogically. She would say, "Ma, which of your friends brainwashed you into getting me married off?" or "Ma, I hope grandmother is not brainwashing you into palming me off to the first person her friend suggests. I am not going to get conned into marrying anyone. You go out of the way to please everyone except me. I have one life and I intend to live it to the fullest. Once one is married, one loses all one's freedom and I am not ready for that."

Such scenes naturally upset me a lot. But, I got over them by rationalizing that Bindu was still an immature kid, so she should be given a long rope. I rarely lost my cool or sulked. Bindu, like her friends, was averse to advice and extremely reactive at times. The redeeming feature was that she would sit with me and enjoy gossiping about the love marriages and affairs from her father's side or Siddu eloping with her boyfriend, Shoaib.

She would say, "Thank God Ma, we have a lot of freedom and bring our friends home, so we won't have to take drastic steps like elopement or far worse, getting pregnant before marriage. It's so frightening." One of Raja's aunts had fallen in love with a man at fourteen and married him after a lot of opposition when she was nineteen. Bindu would tell her grandfather, "Tata (grandfather), at least I am going out with friends after I am past nineteen and that is far better than your cousin, Vaishnavi."

I encouraged our girls to bring their friends home and not hang around street corners or college gates. This way, I felt the girls would have a healthy upbringing where nothing needed to be done secretly. I was convinced that an open culture was being encouraged in the house, little knowing that children will invariably keep something from parents. Here lies the communication gap. Children do not mean to hurt their parents, but they get an insane pleasure in hiding where they went or whom they met. They have their own logic and we have to respect it.

I never understood this psychology, though. I also did not mind the girls going for parties with boys as long as they told us where they were and returned at a reasonable hour. What was reasonable by our perception was too early for the children. The other way round too was also equally true. I did have misgivings about their safety at times, and would naturally worry if they came back too late.

I dinned into their heads from time to time, the need for socio-economic equality in marriage and within followers of the same religion. Bindu and Mohini nodded their heads. Like all teenagers, they had temporary crushes and at times, shared tales about the guys who were chasing them or the affairs their friends had in college.

Mohini would hang on to every word her sister said and the girls would burst into laughter at some private jokes they shared. Generally, the girls included me in many of their chirpy conversations. So I had every reason to be content with the way they were shaping up. If they were drawn to defence officers or men in transferable jobs, I would often remind them that their own careers would come to nothing, so marriage to such people would be impractical. I reminded the girls of this, as I felt Raja would be more than disappointed if their careers took a secondary place to marriage. At times, Mohini said in passing, "Is a career everything? New opportunities will present themselves. But romance can't play second fiddle to a career all the time. The man you end up marrying matters a lot, as he is not a dress to be bought and discarded."

One day, while Bindu was doing her third semester of MBA, she came home pretty upset. Her face showed it. "Mummy, I am pretty confused about arranged marriages. I have lost all faith in them! I told you so long back. You and your kind have outdated ideas in this house." Mohini promptly told her to keep her opinions to herself.

Bindu went on to tell me how Manjeet, her high school friend was married off to an eligible boy, Surjit. Manjeet's father knew of Surjit's family through a good friend of his. After six months of marriage, the newly married couple was having serious problems.

Surjit was the only child of his parents and had left it to them to choose a wife for him. He hardly ever supported Manjeet and was ever ready to please his mother and expected Manjeet to do the same. Manjeet hated her mother-in-law's dominating ways. She expected Manjeet to dance attendance on her all day and socialise with her son in the evenings. She would not hear of her dentist daughter-in-law taking up a job, as it was below their family's dignity. Manjeet felt trapped as she had lost her identity and felt less than human. Bindu finished by adding, "Poor Manjit! Had she found her own spouse, she would have been the happier. That much Ma, for your championing arranged marriages. You're too idealistic. I'm sure you want me to become a doormat in some unknown old-fashioned home in Thandavuru, or better still a village. I am pretty sure your ultimate aim is to see us married off to the first guy you find and hear your peers say things like, 'What a catch Meena has found for her daughter. She's an ideal child and a perfect daughter-in-law.' That will be music to your ears. You are not worried about real freedom for your daughters!"

I was shell-shocked at this outburst and thought for a minute that if Manjeet was in this position, whom could the children blame? Was life about finding faults or finding solutions? I said a little uncertainly, "Bindu, why do you let off without thinking? Are we to try and find the right partners in life or pick faults in the existing systems without having a foolproof alternative? Are you saying parents are dumb and count for nothing and youth alone have all the right solutions?"

"Of course, Ma," said Bindu and laughed when she saw my serious face and said, "I never doubted the wisdom of my parents' generation but, I believe Ma, you get carried away by arranged marriages. You pleased your parents and dumbly accepted their choice. But don't expect us to do that."

I was nonplussed at the turn of the argument and left the room and went into the kitchen to prepare dinner, partly to keep my disturbed mind somewhat occupied and avoid shedding tears in their presence. But my daughter's words were deeply disturbing. Unconsciously, the first signs of stress were showing up. How difficult it would be for the kids,as the time to settle down in marriage came closer, I wondered!

Bindu finished her MBA and was looking out for jobs. Many eligible matches were suggested for her but she told us to wait till she got a job. That also happened. She joined a multinational company as a trainee and completed the six-month probation. Raja and I were proud of Bindu. One Sunday, Bindu walked in after her gym and wanted to chat with me about her own ideas about marriage.

Mohini had to put in her two-bit saying, "Ma, don't get upset about anything. We are only putting our thoughts together and picking your brains. We love talking to you, as you are a think tank." I suggested Raja be roped in too.

"Fine," said the girls.

Raja said, "How about some coffee before my brains are taxed, that too, on a Sunday?" I looked at Bindu who promptly got out of making coffee by saying, "I'm very tired after all the spinning I did at the gym. So, let Mohini make it. Anyway, I don't want coffee." Without waiting a moment Mohini shot back, "Why me? If Bindu won't, I also won't make it. Bindu has you around her little finger. She is your darling, after all."

So poor me, invariably got up from my comfortable rocking chair and made steaming hot coffee and added some biscuits too. I really didn't mind making the coffee. It was the attitude of the girls and how Raja kept quiet about all that was happening…His silence was bugging me and it always did... It wasn't as if they were queens and I was a maid from a slum. I curled up on the divan and said, "Are your friends tying the knot or going steady that you want to clear your ideas with us? I'm proud of you. This open discussion is healthy and desirable."

The discussion went something like this:

Mohini : Papa, normally in movies, books and TV serials, the end is a happy one, but unfortunately, it is far from reality. They tend to misguide us. How many young people's dreams are shattered in real life! This, after all the good wishes and blessings which are showered on young couples on their wedding days... It's all a farce.

Raja	:	Come on my pet, don't get carried away and make sweeping statements. You are still a kid.
Bindu	:	Papa, you are not fair to Mohini. She may be very young but she is fairly mature and down-to-earth. It is true that we can't wish away problems.
Me	:	OK Bindu, you are right. Getting married is important but more important is choosing the right person; but finding Mr. Right is not easy. No proven methods to ensure the right choice exist even today. Choice of marriage is not mathematics. Generally, marriages in our times were happy enough in the age-old system of arranged marriages. The tag of 'right person' depends on the parameters we apply and how the chemistry between two people works.
Raja	:	I don't think the system of choosing partners through arranged marriages has really passed the acid test of successful marriages. Our opinions are based on conjectures and not necessarily on facts. None of us know who is really happy or unhappy and right or wrong. The happiest of marriages may sour with time, and the worst of marriages may turn into healthy relationships. There is an element of gamble in this age-old institution.
Me	:	Raja, why are you talking in riddles? You and I are happy enough. Moreover, everything new is not good either. The success of a marriage is subjective and does not depend on the way two people decide to marry, whether after a long courtship, or as decided by their families.
Mohini	:	Ma, that's not true.
Me	:	What do you mean?
Mohini	:	You have said often that we are happy because we have made compromises. So, is it the right choice? (She banged the table for effect).
Bindu	:	Mummy, do you think you alone made all the sacrifices? How could granny and grandpa stay with us if they hadn't been accommodating? Also, you said that marrying an only child has too many responsibilities which a girl's parents don't give enough thought to before the marriage. Personally, I would not like to get stuck looking after my in-laws all my life. So, it's no to an only child, for me.

Raja : It's true, Bindu. Mummy has put in a lot of effort to make this home happy and welcomed your grandparents wholeheartedly. Please appreciate it and keep that in mind when you pass comments or judge her. That's only fair. I am not perfect either.

But you kids are right too. Your grandfather was in a hurry to see Mummy married. He had an unrealistic confidence that his daughter would adjust in her in-laws' house. Luckily, it worked out for all of us. I don't think your maternal grandfather asked your mother about her dream man. But she proved her father right thanks to her compromises and sacrifices which are not appreciated.

Me : You may be right but whatever kind of marriage we go in for, whether love or arranged,marriage is marriage and the principles remain constant. The people involved have to face realities, find solutions and make suitable changes as and when challenges crop up.

One has to live the journey of marriage and not just build castles in thin air of a fairy tale ending, which you all seem to be building.

Raja : Don't be so serious, Meena. Be more sporting. Bindu, go on and say what you feel.

Bindu : Ma is a dreamer and an idealist. Look at Ramesh and Shilpa. Do you remember how Shilpa was cajoled into marrying that coward of a man just because he is a Chartered Accountant? Sudha Aunty bullied the poor girl into saying yes. They argued that the family was known to the Thakkars. They are our best friends and they mean well. She knows you from birth. Ramesh is smart and well-behaved. Now see what happened! Parents get so carried away when it comes to finding matches.

Raja : I agree with you, Bindu. But how was Suresh Uncle to imagine that Ramesh was going around with Leela. After all, Ramesh lives away from his parents. They have been cheated too. No one knows what he was doing when he was away. For that matter, I wonder if Mummy and I know everything about you and Mohini. We live by trust. Would you disclose to anyone that your friend is having an affair? You will say it is not my business. Anyway, no amount of information is enough when selecting a spouse. We can only try our best and stand by you always, come what may.

Mohini : Papa, in a love marriage, Shilpa would have been spared all this agony. Poor kid! She should never have listened to Sudha Aunty and Suresh Uncle. Or at least she should have had a long engagement. Then Ramesh would have been caught red-handed or at least there would have been a fair chance of knowing that he was going around.

Bindu : Let's not talk of 'ifs' and 'buts'. Our society has too many 'dos' and 'don'ts'. It is one where girls are treated like cattle. Parents expect their so-called darling daughters to be doormats because of their pre-historic mindsets. 'Happiness' has no meaning for parents. I think Dad is no different from our grandfather. He is only marginally better than him. I can't do many things, as he can't find suitable boys for me if I earn a fancy pay. Is marriage the be all and end all of life?

Raja : Very strong words! Yes wise ones, we are dumb and all of you can do no wrong. Best of luck to you! You can find whomsoever you like, but please stick by him. Remember, during courtship both people put on their best behaviour and the truth comes out after the wedding, just as in arranged marriages where there is no time to know each other.

Me : We can't run away from society. Love marriages alone don't hold the key to happiness. Look at Aaruchi. She and Anuraag knew each other for five years. They fought society, parents and all. Still, see what happened to 'Gentleman' Anuraag, who resorted to beating his wife. The poor girl believed she knew Anuraag like the back of her hand!

Raja : Most problems arise from holding back information for irrational reasons.

Bindu : This discussion is getting us nowhere. We can find 'n' number of examples from real life. Ma, as far as I am concerned, I don't mind either way - a love marriage or an arranged marriage. Only, don't brainwash me into saying yes. Find out all you can and I'll meet the guy and then discuss with you without reservations and come to a decision. After all, marriage is a gamble and if it doesn't pay off, we can rectify the mistake always.

Raja : Let us give the alliances that have come up a serious thought and find out all we can and zero down to one or two possible matches for Bindu to choose from.

I devoted a lot of time to scanning the matches that came from advertisements, and those that friends and relatives suggested. The search came to an end when Sheila, a family friend, suggested Rahul Satyamurthy, an engineer with an MBA. His parents lived in Coimbatore after retirement. Raja and I liked Sheila and trusted her suggestion for Bindu, since she knew her since her birth. So Rahul and his parents came to Madras Gymkhana Club and the two families met. Bindu wanted to meet Rahul once more before saying yes. I was worried if Rahul's family would be offended. But Rahul readily agreed and after the second meeting Bindu told us that Rahul and she liked each other. Bindu and Rahul got married two months later in the traditional Hindu way and a fancy reception was held. I was glad all those arguments had helped to clear the air and understanding had followed. The wedding was the talk of the town. I was glad that Bindu had made a good choice.

A year after Bindu's wedding, Mohini left for Ahmedabad to take up a job. She often came home for a holiday. On one such occasion, she and I had the following conversation:

Mohini : Ma, it feels great to be home. I miss Bindu a lot, though. Don't start your Operation Brainwash and your marriage plans for me, or I'll go back to Ahmedabad by the first train.

Me : Sweetheart, your sister is well-settled and happy. We want the same for you.

Mohini : I have to give you credit for a great find in Rahul. Papa and you did a fantastic job! But that doesn't mean every day is Sunday. You look out and so will I, but don't nag me.

Me : Mohini, I am sure you will not do anything stupid. We want your happiness and nothing else. We have to trust each other! You talk as though we, your parents are your foes. All children can't be the same. In a home, we have to live by trust, or else the family will come to grief.

I thought Mohini was a real firebrand who would do well to exercise a little restraint. I began to wonder about the wisdom of having expectations. Mohini is very stubborn and aggressive. Raja and I fight so much about Mohini's marriage and her attitude. She expects us to look out for matches, yet does not take them with the necessary seriousness. She snaps at us or ignores what we say. I just can't figure out all this. She is immature. Well, both the children can't be the same. I just have to be patient and hope the soothsayers are right. No one said she would be a spinster. Mohini always says,"What's the hurry, Ma?" Maybe she is right. I may be overreacting.

One fine day, all this thinking and looking for boys came to an end. It was the first of March. Mohini crept into my bed, cuddled up to me and said, "Ma, I think you have guessed what I want to say. I'm marrying Inayat." The first thing that struck me was that she had chosen to announce her decision when Raja was away on an official tour to Seoul. Was she afraid of Raja? There was pin-drop silence.

Me   : When did you decide? Considering that only a month back you asked me to find out more about Madhur, the boy from Mumbai.

Mohini : When Inayat asked me to marry him in December, I said no way! I can't honestly say when his persuasion made it a yes. I think he is all I am looking for. His parents gave the green signal only this morning. He had a problem convincing them. He moved from Ahmedabad to Calcutta, so leave was a problem too.

Me   : Mohini, have you sorted out some important issues before taking this step – like your religious status and that of your kids?

Mohini : The answer to the first part is yes, I have. I will retain my religion, like Aruna Asaf Ali, and the second - I will cross that bridge when I come to it.

Me   : I'm not competent enough to advise you, but the children's issue needs to be thrashed out. I need to tell Papa.

I felt cold and numb and tossed and turned in bed while Mohini slept like a puppy without a care. All her cares were transferred to me. I thought, "Why me? Why has Mohini done this to me? Did I go wrong somewhere in handling her?"I felt totally betrayed. I needed a bit of fresh air, so I walked in the garden.

Tears rolled down my cheeks. I looked at the stars and wondered if parenting children was only a labour of love without any expectations... When freedom is given, it can't be with strings attached. I dragged myself indoors and heard the phone ring and picked it up on the third ring.

Raja   : Meena?

Me   : Yes... Raja!

Raja	: Yes, Meena darling, what's it? What has happened to your voice?
Me	: Mohini is marrying Inayat, her office colleague.
Raja	: (Long silence)... Meena, I wish I were with you, love... That stupid girl is informing us, not asking us, so leave her alone. We have no choice, so say nothing. I'll call her in the morning. I know how you feel; I'm not happy either.
Me	: Yes Raja, you are right but...
Raja	: Take care love. I'll be with you soon.

I began thinking about my life, studying in Christian institutions, studying the Bible, meeting people and making friends without a thought about who or what they were. My closest friends in college were Naomi and Hazra. Strange, but I never realised then or till now that one was Jewish and the other, a Muslim. They were good friends of mine. They had attended all the functions at my wedding.

My mind wandered as I looked at a family album. It was very unlike me. I was killing time as I waited for Raja to return. Things have changed in more ways than one. Politicians are encouraging fundamentalism for their gain. After all, mankind never started with divisions. The development of the human race has been nurtured and perpetuated by various factors such as religion, culture, geographical proximity, society and so on. Under different umbrellas, we live the journey of life to meet goals of different kinds. But at the same time, these very factors tend to become shackles from which we can't break away. They unify or fragment people at different periods of their lives, causing joy when bonding takes place and unhappiness when they become barriers, as in the case of Mohini and Inayat. I had encouraged the children to visit gurudwaras or churches, but today, an inter-religious marriage seemed like the end of the world.

Why, I wondered? On the one hand, I wanted them to grow up as open-minded people through uninhibited exposure. And on the other, I had closed my mind to interreligious marriages! I was not one to get emotional or illogical, but now, I felt totally ill-equipped to handle my emotions.

Having gone through the album, I looked at Mohini's Baby Book. I had thought a happy, open-minded family like mine had bloomed for years together. Fostering of bonds was inculcated and encouraged in several ways in the girls, in the belief that an intellectual (as we labelled ourselves) is broad-minded in every way. One fools oneself into believing that moving and mingling with different cultural, social, religious and economic groups makes one very open-minded and liberated.

But many put on a façade of being liberal. Even Pandit Nehru disapproved of Feroze Gandhi for his daughter, Indira, for a host of reasons. Double standards are inevitable for humans on minor or major issues.

"We all allude ourselves of being very liberal," I thought, "but it fizzles out and the bubble bursts, when one fine day, the apple of your eye throws a bombshell which shatters your life as if it were a piece of glass. You feel as though a surgeon has cut you up to bleed."

"Oh Raja, how long will you take to reach home?" I said aloud.

I felt that my world had been shattered! What followed were the shock, misery and a big NO, NOT MY CHILD! The woven dreams of years had fallen like a pack of cards and I realised that castles were built on sand. The barriers I shunned in others became justified in my case. I feared the worst and hallucinated about everything that could possibly go wrong in the future. But often, I had no logical arguments, which could change my daughter's mind and I was miserable, as acceptance and understanding were not easily forthcoming within me. After all, time and again, it struck me that my daughter was seeking her happiness. I could not understand why I was hurt. Was it that my ego was hurt?

"You accept under duress, as your own qualities of open-mindedness mock you," I thought, as I dressed to go out for a walk.

Doesn't destiny have the last laugh! One can either accept it with a smile or give vent to emotions. "Don't fight fate, go along with it," a voice from within seemed to say to me. The voice continued, "You did your bit as a parent. Now, let the children do their bit." This catharsis made me feel better and I went to Mohini and said, "What is your plan, Mohini?" She replied, "Let Papa come back and we can talk. After all, Mummy, both of you mean a lot to me."

Together, Raja and I faced the problems which normally crop up before a wedding, and got our beloved daughter married to Inayat. It was great fun to have so many relations who were highly supportive and made the wedding a real happy occasion.

We hoped that the marriages of both our daughters would work out well. Rahul and Inayat could be the gems we were looking for, though choosing them were totally different experiences. We had to stretch our hands farther than we expected, to hug Inayat. But we did it, slowly but surely.

Days rolled into weeks, weeks merged into months and months gave way to a year and Inayat and Mohini celebrated their wedding anniversary. For all my misgivings, I found out that Inayat is as much a human being and a loving husband as Rahul. Beneath all the frightening differences of race, religion and caste, all human beings are the same - average people with the same common cares, like where the next meal is coming from, how to look after the family, how to get on in life and continue to find solutions to problems... just as we, my husband I did to meet the needs of our time. Experience alone is the best teacher. We could not have got a better son-in-law!"

Without giving a lecture, Meena related her first-hand experience of parenting, for which she received a standing ovation from the members of Rainbow and paved the way for many parents.

THE BABY'S FIRST STEP

The last month had been highly traumatic. People came to Moni to express their condolences. The words, "We are sorry to hear the shocking news," buzzed in her ears. Initially, many visitors came, but gradually the numbers trickled down to ones and twos. The atmosphere in the house was unbelievably depressing and exceedingly quiet. People seemed to whisper while talking and walked on tiptoe as if the departed soul would be disturbed if a needle fell on the floor. Moni was left a widow at the age of thirty-two, with not much education which could get her decent employment, or property that would help her to live in reasonable comfort. Additionally, she had to shoulder the responsibility of a fifteen-year-old daughter too.

Both were in shock and totally nervous of facing what the future held for them. The stark realities of life hit them as the days went by. Naturally, financial insecurity nagged Moni who was used to her late husband being the breadwinner. She was comfortable running the house and was never encouraged to study beyond high school by her conservative family who were in a hurry to get her married. Her fears and concerns were totally understandable. It was during this phase of Moni's life that I visited her daily and spent a lot of time holding her hand, reassuring her that the cloud might be very dark but it definitely had a silver lining. On one such afternoon visit, our conversation went something like this:

I : Moni, I don't know how to say this. I feel inhuman touching on such a sensitive topic. I have spent hours wondering whether what I am doing is right or not. I will not continue with what I want to say if you are not ready yet.

Moni: You, and inhuman! Never! It is already four weeks since Vishu left us. I cannot believe it. My life seems like a rudderless boat. Vishu was like a boatman who steered our life. His death is a tragedy I can never overcome.

I : Moni, I think I know how you feel. But reliving the past repeatedly is going to take you nowhere. It only opens up fresh wounds and tears. Tomorrow is the only reality and you have to face it and plan for it too. Collect your thoughts, and whatever help you need from us will be yours. This is my promise.

Moni looked out of the window almost measuring the world and wondering which door would open for her.

Moni: It will always be too soon, so now is as good a time as any to talk and discuss. I am so confused and apprehensive of the future. What I can do I do not know. But I do know I have to struggle from now on to rebuild my life.

I : I feel you should take up a part-time job and qualify further. In two to three years from today, you will be in a position to get a good job, which will give you the money you need and job satisfaction too. What would you like to study? May be you should take an aptitude test.

Moni: I love children and having them around me may fill the loneliness that has surrounded me. Children give me unconditional love when they smile; I feel my life lights up. Also, working mothers need a place where their child can be left with a fair amount of peace and security.

I : Fantastic! You have it all worked out. So why delay! Just open a daycare.

Moni: Will it work out? I don't know.

I : Why not? Working women will be thrilled. Housewives will have a place to leave their children when they want time for themselves. Excellent! You have hit upon the right idea in no time.

Moni: Sanju, I have thought of a name too. It is Happy Hours Day Care. Thanks a ton for helping me.

This conversation helped Moni to take the first major step in rebuilding her life. She opened her daycare and built it brick by brick. She became a second mother to the children who called her Mamma. Today, she is Mamma to the young parents too. Years later, when her grandson was born I asked her how she felt and she said that all the children in her crèche would go back to their homes, leaving her to lonely evenings, but her grandchild would always be with her.

Five years after the crèche was started, we were chatting over a cup of coffee. The gist of the talk was interesting. Moni analysed her experiences and went on to share them with me.

Moni: Sanju, most women have a strong desire to be mothers and take care of children physically and mentally. This often involves making a lot of sacrifices. This is done willingly as the umbilical connection is very strong. This giving of unconditional love by a woman makes her the pillar and cornerstone of society. She instils values and traditions in the child while feeding spoonful's of rice and narrating stories from history and mythology. This is when the foundation is laid by each generation for the next.

I   : Moni, you are right as always. Until recently, a woman's life spun around the home and she was happy enough in a joint family. She got the support of other women who helped to bring up the child or children so she could leave them and visit her parental family or for that matter, go for a movie or for functions. Group participation and living among cousins helped a child develop its personality. Problems related to an only child were taken care of. Not everything about a joint family was good. But the children's grandparents helped to balance and ensure a healthy flow of communication. They gave advice and helped solve problems. So people like you were not required then.

Moni: Sanju, people like me came into existence when the joint family began to make way for the nuclear family. Women began to transform themselves with education and that sharpened their thinking. They began to leave home to supplement the income or for the self-satisfaction of using their knowledge and skills. At meetings with parents, many parents who come to me discuss issues about working women and the problems that go with it.

This shift was not easy for women because they faced resistance not only from the men in the family, but also female relatives who made things difficult for them by showing their envy through taunts and a continuous increase in demands on them.

But determined women were loath to give up on their new-found freedom easily. They liked it, savoured it and held on to it at all costs. It dawned on them that the demands of their jobs could be met fully only if they had a support system to take care of their children. They experimented with the idea of leaving their kids with good friends or willing neighbours in exchange for help which they could render while coming home, like getting groceries or vegetables. Soon, they began to pay for this help and this practice led to the birth of crèches or day care centres. I am glad Sanju that I can help working women. I feel sorry for the mothers who have to prepare lunch for themselves and their husbands by dawn and get their sleeping children to the crèche.

One day, Moni was crying when I happened to drop in. I was worried. After some coaxing she said that one of the parents of a child in her day care had insulted her. She was told that she was just an ayah, a paid governess. I was shocked and calmed her down and told her to just ask those parents to leave if they couldn't appreciate the hours and effort she was putting in towards the upbringing of their child. The work she was doing was invaluable.

Parenting is done in a crèche to a large extent, but in a much more professional manner, than at homes. This has some added advantages like the objective viewing of problems in children's behaviour. We know this is difficult for parents, as their emotional involvement in their own child is very high.

Let us take the example of Rahul, a two-year-old. He is an only child, who hates milk and gives any amount of trouble to his mother to drink it. The mother fusses so much over the ritual of drinking milk that both mother and child dread it. The mother sometimes whacks her son when he throws a tantrum. Very often, both end up in tears. In a crèche, this kind of problem gets sorted out very easily. In a group, Rahul toes the line. He joins his friends in drinking milk at fixed times with less resistance and more fun. Just being with the other children and eating and drinking with them helps an only child enjoy the company of other children.

I got a call from Moni one morning saying, "Sanju, I'm really happy today. Sahil called me up from Dubai to tell me that he has come first among all the sections of his class in the International School. His mother, Anagha added that I had played an important role in his formative years."

I said, "Moni, I'm so happy for you. Life has its ups and downs." One happy set of parents had even taken Moni for a holiday with them as they came to treat her as a part of their family for doing an excellent job of looking after their son, who had come to her crèche as an eight-week-old baby.

This is the journey of a brave woman who has rehabilitated herself. The crowning glory in her life was when my grandson, a three-month-old infant joined her family of children in the daycare. She said on the phone, "Sanju, when I started my venture in 1985, I never believed I would be holding Neal in my arms in 2004. Thanks for the pleasure and privilege."

PARANJALA - THE POLITICIAN

Ensconced in the backseat of her chauffeur-driven Opel Astra, Paranjala Munim took out the mirror from her handbag and touched up her face. She was very pleased with what she saw. It was a smart, pleasing face which often turned many heads. But she was really glad that more people admired her for the brains behind the pretty face.

She had been championing many social causes related to women, their problems and hardships. She empathized with rural and urban women while weighing their problems and aspirations, and often came out with reasonable and practical solutions. She almost never made false promises. She thought of Arun Malhotra, her opponent. Time and again, he promised the moon. He won elections by doling out incentives or cash to the illiterate electorate and not by keeping to his promises.

Paranjala wanted to be an honest representative of her constituency and show her people what she had done for five years and then seek their support to be re-elected. Arun had once told her, "Paranjala, don't slog so much. It does not pay." She only smiled and said, "Maybe you are right. Let me try it my way." She meticulously worked towards her goals. To give an example, she identified the areas of concern and prioritized them. She wrote out street plays and advertisements to spread the message of cleanliness and health. Next, she sent trainers to address groups of men and women about the advantages of potable water. These went up on television, radio and in street plays. They were enacted in schools and college. Visual impact was the trick and it worked so well that water-borne diseases had reduced considerably. She also took up the cause of woman's education and spread the message of 'Each one teach one.'

On her thirty-fifth birthday, she got the news of winning her first election as an MLA . Later, she became an MP . People praised her honesty and placed great hopes in her. It was a few days before the parliament was to be convened. She was walking on air as she climbed the steps to the legislative assembly. Her Dad called and said, "Paru, my child I am proud of you. Be good, do good. It is the difficult, but correct path. I will expect nothing less."

Now,in the car, she looked at her planner and realized that in the next three hours, she would be chairing a meeting on an interesting subject. It would be tabled in the parliament later and hopefully, be passed as a bill. The subject was, 'Homemakers to get a weekly-off by law.' Constructive deliberation would help move it in the right direction. That morning, she was being interviewed by a journalist of a leading newspaper.

She got down from the car and ran up the steps leading to the entrance of a brand new commercial building in Nehru Place, one of Delhi's poshest localities, in which her office was located. She went to the elevator, past the glass doors that opened automatically. It suddenly occurred to her, "Automation has helped cut costs by reducing manual labour - like eliminating the doorkeeper and lift man. But on second thoughts, glass doors open automatically but the smiling face and greetings of the doorman are missing. His absence rings a bell and we all long for the human touch."

Her mind stopped wandering on seeing her secretary, Leena. She briefed her on the first meeting and ushered in Manpreet who represented 'Shakti', a well-established women's magazine. The interview started well with Paranjala answering the questions with ease and a ready smile. The fifth question took her by surprise.

Manpreet : Ma'am, there is a section of women who believe MPs would be doing irreparable harm to the housewives.

Paranjala : Why do they feel that way, Manpreet?

Manpreet : Ma'am, the women seem convinced that they are being misunderstood and their roles are totally undervalued. They are livid at the politicians who, they think are treating women as non-entities. They also feel the politicians are living in the misnomer of knowing that they know what is best for everyone and can decide for everyone.

Paranjala : I assume that they think we take them to be dumb, and we feel that by passing the bill we are doing them a great favour.

Manpreet : Exactly! And these women are asking who has the right to determine their welfare, the MPs or they themselves? So I am asking you, who do you support - the women who are outraged at this step or the parliamentarians? One lady told me, "The government can't protect us against rape; but can condescendingly give us a weekly-off."

Paranjala gulped the coffee Leena had brought them and said, "Manpreet, I would like to defer this interview till the weekend. The issue is a sensitive one and I need to think about your feedback and the answer to the question you have asked me. It has to be handled with kid gloves or there will be a volcanic eruption... I need to consider all possible points of view to avoid flared tempers. Thank you very much. Sorry for cutting the interview short but I am sure you understand..."

She asked Leena to call for the car and rushed down. The driver said, "Where to, Madam?" "Home," said Paranjala. Then she called up the organisers on her mobile and postponed the morning's meeting to 9.30 pm, late evening. The audience would include a few MPs, NGOs and professionals.

A minute later, she said, "Suresh, turn the car and drive to the farmhouse." "Right, Madam," said Suresh. As the car passed the all too familiar roads in Mehrauli, she noticed women going about their daily activities like buying vegetables, meat, fruits, groceries etc.

She looked back on her life and thought, "I sure am missing out on a lot of fun,like chatting away with shopkeepers, vendors and hawkers... It makes us and the shopkeepers feel so much at home when we ask them, "Sethji, how did your daughter fare in her board exams?" He answers with his chest out with pride, "Did I not tell you that she got eighty percent? Have a sweet.""

When her mother had died, reminisced Paranjala, the milkman too had cried as if he had lost his kin. "I miss such moments as they enrich our lives and re-establish our faith in each other in this material world... But you can't have it all. Many would give their right arm to be in my shoes."

Her mind came back to the immediate problem which had disturbed her considerably. She wondered, "Was there any truth in what Manpreet had shared? Undoubtedly, women are housewives first and foremost, and all their other roles follow. So why are we, politicians differentiating between working women who have careers and those who spend their time working in the house? It is something like the divide between the haves and the have-nots. Whether a woman brings in a second income or is the sole breadwinner, or takes care of the icing on the cake, or spends all the time building her home as a housewife, she is the pillar of her home. The supposedly humble housewife is surely not a second-class citizen! The home is a woman's heart and soul and she belongs there and gives it her hundred percent to see it bloom and prosper." Paranjala went back to her own life and thought, "I am happiest where I belong and am wanted the most, which is my home. Home is not the four walls;it is where my son Ravi, daughter Namrata and husband Manish are. I wouldn't exchange this happiness for anything else in the world. Everything else is secondary to it; fame, money and so on."

She reached her farmhouse,'Sunshine' and slowly entered her living room where they had a number of parties for close friends who were neither politicians nor professionals. Manish, her husband, a chartered accountant, was very fond of his friends and entertained them there. Their parties were popular because of the warmth the inmates exuded. Paranjala and Manish had a circle of intelligent, well-to-do and not so well-to-do friends who had discussions on different subjects each time they met and all of them enjoyed themselves thoroughly. Often, Namrata, Ravi, Paranjala and Manish spent memorable weekends on the farm. At such times, Paranjala was not an advocate or an MP but a wife, mother and a hostess. She cooked each and every meal and took care of all the needs of her family.

"Can a labour of love be related to rights, laws and demands? No way!" she concluded. "But on the other hand, is a woman really equipped to fight for what she wants?" She continued to delve deeper. "Is she empowered to get what she desires and fight for herself? I guess so! Are parliamentarians the right people to handle issues related to the emotionally sensitive areas of her life? No, not necessarily. Do they really crusade for women's welfare or fatten their vote bank at the expense of treading on sensitive issues? Gender discrimination and capitalizing on it is not my cup of tea," she thought. "That seems to be the crux of the matter that is causing so much turmoil in the hearts of women and that's what they are giving vent to."

"Why am I breaking my head over this important issue alone? Let me get Sri and Simran over and clear the cobwebs. They are well-read, mature individuals who wish me well and are my harshest critics too. They don't bat an eyelid in calling a spade a spade. She called them and opened a book and on the last page found what she had noted some time ago. It said, "In a democratic system, MPs must belong to a party but must cut across party lines to get different view-points if the situation warrants it. That apart, to be accepted as a competent parliamentarian, one must get as many different opinions as possible. This is one way of being respected in the world of politics where high standards have to be set and adhered to. In this way of life, one should find ways of serving society and the country and not enriching oneself through immoral means." She felt better after reading it.

Paranjala was so lost in her thoughts that she was oblivious to the arrival of her friends, which surprised them. Sri and Simran, Paranjala's closest friends, admired their friend's achievements. Both of them were housewives. Sri had done her post-graduation in Mass Communication and had worked for some time before giving it up when she got married. She and Vimal were proud of their children and it showed in the way they discussed them.

Sri and Simran went across to the sofa where Paru, as they called Paranjala, was sitting. Paru suddenly came back to the present with a bang and welcomed them. She called for some ice-cream and said aloud, "It is so unlike me to cancel everything and come to my hideout at this time of the day. But I'm happy to be here to pick your brains." Simran said, "My! We haven't met in a week. Paru, I'm glad you called, though the timing, I agree, is unusual for you." Sri said, "Why are you buttering the future PM? They all laughed but Paranjala's preoccupation did not escape them.

She got down to business with no further delay and put her thoughts and concerns across to her friends for their reactions and comments. They heard what the journalist had asked and Paru's feelings. Simran said, "Paru, you won't like what I'm going to say, but I will say it since you asked us and expect total honesty. You politicians often exploit situations to promote your own ends. Politicians couldn't care less whether people involved, like us, are made pawns. I agree that a woman, like any other member of a joint or nuclear family needs to relax and have time to devote to herself. But this does not give politicians the right to split hair and say that housewives need to be given a weekly-off through legislation. A politician's mind, on an average, Paru, is a devil's workshop, looking for new areas to build vote banks to ensure their election and fill their pockets at every opportunity. Are we to be pawns on a chessboard while they make moves at their whims and fancies to promote themselves?"

Sri piped in, "Yes Paru, I agree with Simran that politicians are taking the law into their hands. A home is not made of bricks and cement but the inmates who have hearts, souls and feelings. A woman makes a home, like you have made yours. Your penthouse or farm comes to life when the family is there. The woman is the heart and pulse of her home. How can anyone decide what she wants? She alone can decide, whether she is a career woman or a homemaker. I wonder who came out with this brilliant one that housewives need to be protected in the form of entitling them to a weekly-off! I hope not you!

Paru, are you trying to say that the women who stay at home and make their home their life and soul are to be referred to as 'housewives'? Each one of us is a homemaker irrespective of our social welfare activities and careers. Once a woman gets married, the couple set up home and the woman manages the home and children, and much later, the grandchildren. This way, the family grows and prospers. She tries to meet the needs of the family on all fronts. She gives unstinting hundred percent without expecting too much in return. All that she wants is understanding and love.

So what is all this trash you are talking about? Discussions about a housewife! Why walk all over her life telling her how to relax and for how long? What you legislators will get in exchange is votes and better positions. Paru, you should not get into all this. You should be far above the petty, small politicians we see on a daily basis."

"A single woman often lives in the family she is born into," Simran decided to add her bit. "There too, she gives to the family hundred percent and works on all seven days of the week. Young girls who lose their mothers, often take on the role of homemakers. Thus, we see that single as well as married women love their homes and give it their all. My husband, Jaggu would laugh his sides out if there was talk of a weekly-off for housewives. He would say, 'Sweetheart, who stopped you from taking an off from your household chores whenever you wanted to?'"

"My husband will also say something similar," piped in Sri. Simran ignored her and continued, "My husband thinks I am the queen of my home which is my domain totally. How true this is Paru!" Paru did not comment. "We can decide what to do and when to do something and most importantly, whether something should be done or not. What are we being promised by the parliament? We have to live our lives in our homes the way we want to. If we are not living life as we want to, then no one else can help us to do it. A woman has to manage her home efficiently within the framework of her family. She can't work herself to the bone and then go about like a martyr. She must manage her time well, involving all her dear ones. Very often we give up our powers of decision making and reduce ourselves to little more than domestic helps, at the beck and call of everyone else. Look at poor Leela. Her teenage children throw it at her that she is after all their mother and should take charge of everything. It is totally Leela's fault. She has to get out of her own emotional shackles. She is a human being playing her varied roles cut out for her by nature and not a God."

"Yes Paru, Simran is totally right."

Paranjala felt there was a lot in what her friends candidly expressed.

"You have opened my eyes to what you feel. But wouldn't a woman, in the name of sacrifice and compromise have her freedom curtailed?"

"No Paru," said Sri, "your sentence is not quite right. She ought to be assertive and make her own decisions." Paru had a confused look. Sri noticed it and said, "Let me explain this with an illustration. Let us take the example of Meena, a mental weakling who wanted to go for a walk every morning. Her teenage children and her husband questioned her as to how she could go for a walk when their lunch had to be packed or hot breakfast needed to be made. Raju, Meena's son told her, "You have the whole day to yourself. You are at home all day. Must you choose to walk in the morning when you need to attend to the kitchen?'" I think Meena should have done something. She just gave in and muttered to herself. Then how could she say that others were walking all over her? She shouldn't have been soft and got trampled underfoot. She should have trained and persuaded the members of her family to help her in the home and accommodate her needs too. Ideally, if Meena happens to go for a movie or a coffee party, she should expect not glum faces on her return, but a smile and better still, a cup of tea. She needs not a weekly-off, but time for herself to spend as she likes or needs to." Paranjala's bright eyes sparkled as she nodded her understanding.

"Sri," said Paranjala, "you are trying to say that no one should undermine the role of the wife or mother or sister by saying, 'What were you doing all day? Only going for a sale or buying groceries...'"

"Right," Sri nodded, "Earning money is not the bottom line for evaluating a woman and her contribution. We have to appreciate that all the time the homemaker is working and trying her hardest to keep each member of the family happy. They must appreciate her selfless efforts in making each one happy and be sensitive to it."

"What I can't understand Paranjala," said Simran, "is how external agencies have decided to crusade on issues which catch their fancy. Each woman has to know what is best for her and has to work towards it. Family members have to be supportive of the homemaker and not the parliament. Can you just imagine this scene: Pushpa plans to go for an afternoon movie. Her husband Balu calls up to say, 'Push, I'm bringing three people over for lunch today. Make sure there is some beer in the fridge. Bye! See you later, around one-thirty.' Is Pushpa going to say, 'Remember, it's my day off today, Balu, and I'm going for a movie... ' or will she understand Balu's requirement and postpone the movie? If the tickets are already bought, she may take care of the lunch and go for the movie. She has to decide on the best solution." Paranjala played with a pencil and asked, "My dear oracles, how will rural women react to the parliament giving them a day off?"

Simran replied, "I don't know too much. The simpletons that they are, they believe the house is their temple. It gives them immense pleasure. Their homes are not built on sand but on sterner stuff. A lot of distribution of work takes place and unity is the strength of their homes. They will find their own solutions as problems crop up. A village woman is unlikely to seek legal redress or political help to fight her domestic battles. Each one of us became a housewife when we entered the threshold of our home by putting the auspicious right foot ahead first. Among our Christian friends, the groom carries his bride across the threshold to symbolise their entry into their home they are making. So the government, Paru, doesn't confer the title of a housewife to a woman when she enters the institution of marriage."

Paranjala looked out of the window. She saw some farmers' children coming back from college. She thought, "Almost all girls dream of a home of their own for social, traditional and biological reasons. Running a home is a labour of love on which we can't put a value. A woman faces many kinds of challenges in her lifetime; as a daughter, sister, daughter-in-law, mother, mother-in-law and grandmother. It requires all her sagacity, patience and sensitivity to rise to the various challenges from time to time. Her inner strength and power are within the home and not outside.

Sri broke into her thoughts and said, "Paru, hypothetically, if the government passes such a law, the question that will arise is, who is to enforce it?"

"Okay. You both know what you are talking about and I need to put on my thinking cap. I have to face an intelligent and intellectual audience like you two lassies. Thanks a ton for your honest opinion. Pretty cutting, I must say. You tore me to pieces!" Rising, Paru added, "Let's have some lunch now. I'm famished. Listening to you is an exhausting experience!" They all laughed.

Paranjala had a pencil in her hand and drew faces on a paper. Then she tore it. She took stock of the situation. It suddenly struck her that the problems of the well-heeled could be very different to those of the poor. She wasted no time in calling the two women domestics who worked in the farmhouse. She asked them the questions she had on her mind. These simple, uneducated, yet well-informed women were surprised at their mistress. In their local language, they told her that many rights, like the right to equal sharing of property with brothers existed for them only on paper. The treatment they got at home depended on their father and brothers and not the law. Loving brothers may help them, but not the lawyer. Also, it took very long and was useless. "In the same way," one of them said, "we cannot get a holiday from the government. I can come to work when I want and enjoy when I want. But, I don't have that luxury anyway. It is only for the rich, Memsahib." At the end of the conversation, Paranjala felt the need for a chat with her husband for his male point of view. She called him up and apprised him of the brain-picking she had done. Manish had nothing to add and said, "Best of luck, darling."

Now, fully armed with different points of view, Paranjala prepared her speech for the evening. She knew only one thing that she couldn't let herself down. She had to be honest to herself and her work. Her theme would be, 'A women is not a puppet in anyone's hands but is the only one who can empower herself.'

Later in the day, her meeting with women of different age groups, from different walks of life and strata of society was a thumping success. It was a unique experience for Paranjala who spoke as a human being and a woman without any other adjective attached to her. She spoke from the heart, touching a chord in her audience. Her approach was a little off-beat for a lawyer and politician. She took the stand that a woman or man has their roles cut out for them when relating to the home. A healthy home adds meaning to the lives of its members and vice versa. Each member in the family depends on the other for support and strength and most of all seeks acceptance from them. This interdependence spreads peace and happiness which exudes a spirit of give and take. Legislation can't make a woman take a day off each week, but the love and understanding of the family can. Legislation can only lead to strife and internal disharmony as it has its limitations. The rural woman would not be affected by the bill. She has to, may be, wait a little and the urban woman can help her in this evolution.

The punch line in her interactive session was that a woman needs space and time for herself, to pursue different interests, like going to a library, watching a play, playing a game or going to observe nature in the hills or near the sea. You can't bargain like a union leader where love dwells. This is what a home is all about. Her final sentence was, "Just as stone walls do not a prison make, so too, parliaments don't a woman liberate."

Paranjala got a standing ovation and became the darling of the press and its readers. DD1 telecast the meeting live. Manpreet sent her flowers – very unusual for a seasoned and aggressive scribe like her, with a note, 'Ma'am, we are proud to have a statesman in you and not a mere politician.'

When Paranjala came home on that memorable day, her husband, Manish said it with flowers and a big hug. She felt that the shackles of a politician were not going to throttle her public life. Later, at night, her children, Namrata and Ravi said, "Congrats Ma! You deserve a weekend in Bangaram Island. Here is your ticket!" Paranjala felt elated for having such a loving family and wished all families were like hers.

She closed her eyes and saw a rose bush full of thorns. The flowers crowned them all. She got the message and smiled. She had lost the goodwill of many a politician but was re-elected by a thumping majority.

MERRY
WIVES AT
A PARTY!

The party was in full swing at Shiva, their dream house. The hosts, Sudheer and Uma Sharma lived in a palatial house in Banjara Hills, an up-market locality in the ancient city of the nawabs (aristocrats) of Hyderabad. Sudheer was a captain on commercial vessels with a Singapore-based company. The couple chose to settle down here because they fell in love with the ancient culture and history that offered exotic cuisine and most importantly, a cosmopolitan atmosphere. They had come to attend a wedding a few years back and were moonstruck by the people and the city.

What is special about the city, one may well ask? Beauty lies in the eyes of the beholder and the city's simplicity touches the hearts of one and all. The couple believed the rugged hills of the Deccan plateaux in the background would add a mystic touch to their dream house.

The party was in the sprawling living room. It had all the trappings of wealth very subtly displayed with soft lighting, artistic flower arrangements and precious artefacts collected from the countries Sudheer and Uma had visited. All in all, Shiva was the owner's pride and the envy of many guests.

This evening, there were about thirty invitees. Of them, seventeen women were single, as their hard-working husbands were on the high seas, earning their bread and butter. For a few of them, there was the proverbial 'girl at every port' too. This group was closely knit, as their way of life was identical and they faced common problems. All the husbands were in and out of the blue waters, so the women enjoyed a high degree of interdependence. They often socialized into the wee hours.

The extremely well-dressed women wore ensembles and accessories that were trendy and exclusive. They were all having a great time dancing, singing, catching up on all the gossip and not to forget, pulling each other's leg. The much-needed frolic and fun provided the silver lining to their lives. The music was loud and jazzy. Almost everyone was swaying to the music on the improvised dance floor. Those who sat out were tapping away their well-manicured feet, encased in footwear bought at outrageous prices in Europe and America. Most of them were compulsive shoppers, much to the envy of their non-Merchant Navy friends. Among themselves too, there was a lot of one-up-man-ship and catching up with the Joneses.

Neela made a late entry as usual. She invariably enjoyed the undivided attention of the menfolk when she entered late by an hour or so. She knew she made heads turn. Today, she looked stunning in her white French chiffon sari and the pearl white choker her hubby had specially got her from Japan for her last birthday. Even after she drove up to the parking, she delayed her entry a little longer, lingering over parking her white BMW, an anniversary gift from her darling husband. She knew Vicky spoilt her totally by indulging in every whim of hers. But why not! She felt that it was the least he could do for an excellent wife like her who made sure he had no worries when he was sailing. She was a great daughter-in-law and a doting mother. For some uncanny reason, she missed Vicky badly today and wished she were walking on his arm rather than alone to the party. He always, she remembered fondly, admired her in white and called her 'My angel in White'. "Oh darling, I must talk to you soon after the party," she decided, as she ran a brush through her hair. She walked in saying, "Hi folks, sorry to be late. The kids..." The host and hostess welcomed her with a warm hug and said, "Neela, no excuses. We know you only too well. It's a wonder that you catch a flight on time!" Neela laughed and moved on to say hi to all her friends and got chatting with the others.

Somewhere, in the deep recesses of the house, a phone was ringing away incessantly. Someone perked up an ear. He tried to wave off the sound. Finally, he went to the phone.

"Hello."

"Sudheer?"

"He's outside somewhere. Can I take a message?"

"No. Please call Sudheer. It's urgent, an emergency. I'm calling from Mumbai."

"Okay, okay. Sudheer…, Sudheer… a call for you. Mumbai. Come fast."

"Hurry up!"

*   *   *   *   *   *

Sudheer picked up his drink and went dancing to take the call. He hoped his leave was not being cut short.

"Hello."

"Sudheer, is that you?"

"Yes."

"Gulu here, calling from the duty room. Tragedy of tragedies! I believe Neela is at your place."

Downing his drink, Sudheer said, "Yeah! What happened?"

"Bad news, I'm afraid. Break it gently to her. Vicky's ship seems to have sunk. Off the Liberian coast."

"Jesus! O my Gosh! I can't believe it!"

"Last call for help came in at zero four hours GMT. Since then we have not been able to reach them. No wreck or survivors spotted."

"Oh no! What a place to…" Anand walked up quietly to Sudheer and raised his eyebrows. Sudheer put his finger to his mouth in reply. "I'm sure you'll do all you can, Gulu."

"We tried our best. Sorry, no luck. The air-sea search has been called off. Sorry. Bye."

"Bye."

Sudheer had a quick discussion with Anand on the course of action. They decided that the best option was to break the news in stages. It was one thing to take charge of a crisis on a ship as the Captain, and totally another to gently deal with the wife of a colleague and dear friend. Now he had to handle a widow. "What do I say? How do I break the news? What am I expected to say?" thought Sudheer. He was numb and felt inept at handling this extremely delicate and sensitive situation.

"How will Neela take it? Will she be hysterical, or worse still, faint? Oh, why her? The heavens were envious of her good luck. What a couple she and Vicky made! Really made for each other!"

He remembered the time they had won the Couple of the Day Award at the Maritime Day celebration. "Neela is such a fun-loving person. Fate is more than unfair to her. In a split-second, it has taken away all that mattered to her." As thoughts raced through his mind, he pulled himself together and moved towards the guests.

He raised his hand and said, "One sec, friends." He stopped the music to get their attention. "There could be some earth-shattering news or nothing alarming. Some ship may be in trouble. Before I could get the details, the line was dead." He couldn't believe that he was actually doing all this. Vick, dear Vick! He wished he did not have to go through this torture. He would do anything to have him here, alive and kicking! What Vicky must have gone through when the ship was capsizing he could well imagine, but, what agony he himself was going through now, Vick would never know.

Instantly, a hush fell on the merrymakers. All smiles turned into frowns and not a whisper was heard. There was pin drop silence. The impending doom seemed to creep into the very bones of the women who were huddled together in their hour of adversity, which they could certainly sense. The ladies whose husbands were on board, looked ghastly. Undoubtedly, it had to be one of their husbands. Only, they did not want to guess who the unfortunate one was. None of them believed the bit about the line getting cut.

The waiting certainly extended the period of hope for each of them. Seema started shedding tears and sniffed into her delicately embroidered handkerchief. She panicked easily and was a bundle of nerves. Usually, she went to pieces when her husband Sanju delayed calling her by a few days or her son fell ill. Now, she felt she couldn't take the tension any more. She would collapse. The waiting was killing her.

Leena silently chanted the Hanuman-Chalisa which was chanted during adversity to draw strength to face doom. Lord Hanuman helped dispel fear in the hearts of humans if they repeated the forty verses as often as possible and particularly when in trouble. Neela glanced at Leena and shook her head in pity and thought that prayers were not going to help. Whatever had happened couldn't be reversed. She remembered the saying, 'Where reason ends, faith begins'. "If Leena gets solace, let her pray. Each to their own! Que sera sera, what will be will be." Neela marvelled at her own presence of mind.

Each one of the ladies kept hoping for the best and thinking, "Not me. I can't take it! Oh God, let it not be me! Please spare me. I have not consciously harmed anyone."

All the women's faces were drawn and pinched. Each second of waiting was taking its toll and they were reduced to ghosts of what they had been just moments earlier. "Oh God, this is killing," said Pammy to herself. "Why can't we get it over with? At least the mental torture will end." The silence said it all – the mood, the dread, the hope and the fear which gripped the wives. The axe would fall on one of their heads.

Neela broke the deathly silence and opined that it may be a minor accident on the ship and their heroes would be back. "I am going to fetch a drink," she said. She looked at Anand and asked him to make her a martini. Anand readily obliged and felt she would need it badly. Moreover, he had something to occupy him. He remembered the last party Neela and Vick had for their anniversary and the fun they had till well past two in the morning. Neela had looked ravishing in a midnight blue chiffon dress and the glittering diamonds at her neck. She had been the heart and soul of the evening. He sighed as he thought how merciless life could be! Then a thought struck him – he should increase his insurance. God knows who the next victim of death would be!

Sudheer looked at his watch and announced in a flat voice, "Let me see if Mumbai has any more news. Let us hope the lines are okay." He closed the door behind him. Neela thought that the doors of life were closing for one of them.

Each second seemed like an age. The finality of death and its supremacy over mortals hammered into the chaotic minds of the people present.

Uma moved around restlessly, picking up an empty glass or a used napkin. Her mind kept saying, "Sudheer, hurry up! How long are we to wait? Her heart beat very fast, when she realized that it was the 13th of March. "Sudheer always mocked my belief in superstitions. See what has happened now," she thought.

As Neela came out of the rest-room, she couldn't help noticing the empty glasses at the bar and the men talking in hushed tones and looking in her direction. Were they looking at her in particular, she wondered. No, no. Why should they? "I am imagining too much. After all, it can be any one of us whose husbands are away? Didn't the face reader say, 'You will both live to see your grandchildren'? He had to be right!"

"Vicky would laugh if he saw you like this, like a jellyfish reliving what soothsayers had to say," said an inner voice. Then she remembered during Dushera, Ma Durga had blessed her. The garland had fallen into Neela's arms when she had closed her eyes to seek Ma Durga's blessings. She reassured herself thus, and felt a bit bad, laughing at Leena chanting the mantra.

After what seemed an eternity, Sudheer returned. His face gave away nothing. All eyes were riveted on his ashen face. He almost dragged his feet to delay going through the hateful task in store for him. His shoulders drooped from the burden thrust on him.

He walked towards Neela. He hated what he was about to do with each step he took. He held both Neela's hands and said softly,

"Neela, Vicky..." Neela blinked and pinched herself.

"No, it can't be!" she whispered to herself. "My Vicky can't leave me. He is too young, only 33. There must be a mistake."

All the other ladies – secretly relieved, but skilfully hiding their feelings – came round to her. It is easy to be compassionate when it is someone else! Neela stared at the ceiling and silent tears streamed down her pretty cheeks. She hated women who exhibited tears in public, so she wiped them and stared in the distance. The children needed her now. She had to break this earth-shattering news to Bob who was only five and Kirti, eight and her in-laws.

"How do I tell them?" she thought. "Will the kids understand death and its permanence? Poor things! They don't deserve all this. Time will take care of them. And me, who will? The one who did is not there for me anymore."

Her heart said, "Neela, no one is above the will of God, but time is the best healer." Neela could imagine life from now on without Vicky. It was bound to be a long, endless tunnel of darkness.

With trembling fingers, she picked out the car keys from her bag. It was the solid link she had with Vicky and held on to them for dear life. She wished Vicky would call and say it was a prank to test her love.

"How naïve can I get," she thought, "My Vick would never do that."

She looked at Sudheer and said, "I must go now." She turned to the others, looked at the lucky ones and moved to the door. Sudheer insisted on driving her home.

"No thank you, Sudheer. I can, or rather, have to manage on my own. Now I have no one to share my life with. I have no one to love and fight with." She broke down and said, "Maybe you should come with me and break the news at home, while I get a grip on myself. My poor in-laws don't deserve all this. I do hope they have not heard anything yet."

Sudheer turned the ignition and the engine sprang to life. "If only somebody could spring her Vicky back to life! Oh no! It could never be!" she thought. She could only see Vicky in the cold clutches of death, succumbing after putting up a brave fight. "Whom did he think of as he breathed his last? Me, the kids or himself? Oh God! It doesn't matter now. I have all my life to relive the past."

With no Vicky to be her perpetual shadow, as he had been through thick and thin for thirteen years and thirteen days, she felt stone-cold. She took out Vick's snap that was on the dashboard. She sensed that his spirit would never leave her.

"May be there is some truth in the old superstition of the unlucky 13. Today is 13th March, a Friday," she thought as she opened the car door to enter her house with Sudheer's help and begin a new chapter.

The party had turned out to be a nightmare for Neela and the events of the evening had left a deep scar on her life. The business of living had to go on, but she was scared of parties and stormy seas. The void in her life was making it meaningless and mechanical. She wondered for whom the house was being kept in order. There was no Vicky to playfully find fault with her housekeeping. There was no one to tease her on her penchant for frequently rearranging the house.

"Why, for whose sake!" she thought. She cried often. One day, on Vicky's first death anniversary, to be precise, she realized she was dressing sloppily. She began introspecting.

Did losing a husband mean leading a lousy life? Would she be a dead man's wife forever? Would Vick, looking down from wherever he was, approve of her present state? The answer was a resounding NO. In that moment, she decided to pick up the loose ends of her life, tie them up and start life all over again.

In a few months, she got a job with a travel agency. Some six weeks later, Akaash Sharma walked in to plan a business trip to Korea. He did more than that. She had walked straight into the void in his heart and he wooed her till she accepted him with no reservations. He had lost his wife in an accident a month after they were married.

Vicky was Neela's past, one she never forgot and treasured undoubtedly, but Akaash became her present and her future.

"If you try to please everyone, you will please no one.
It is impossible to lead your life for others' happiness."

— Sudha Murty, Wise & Otherwise

www.ingramcontent.com/pod-product-compliance
Lightning Source LLC
Chambersburg PA
CBHW031239260626

47169CB00007B/2379